LEGACY OF WRATH

A HIP-HOPALYPTIC SUPERHERO THRILLER

SHEER WILL

LEGACY OF WRATH:

A HIP-HOPALYPTIC SCI-FI ACTION THRILLER

Published by Sheer Will Productions

Sheerwill1@sheerwillproductions.com

Philadelphia, PA 19140

Copyright © 2014 by William G. Reynolds

Second Edition, 2022

Library of Congress Control Number: 2022909336

ISBN: 979-8-218-39423-3

Edited by Artizann

Cover art concept, graphics and design by Sheer Will

Printed and bound in the United States of America.

Visit us on the web at www.sheerwillproductions.com

To my mother, for being my gateway onto the planet, my first teacher and for showing me unconditional love.

To my children, for being the fingerprints of my existence and the beautiful melodies of my spirit.

And to all the beacons of creativity from the past, the present and the future...

I AM BECAUSE WE ARE.

PROLOGUE

The beginning of the gospel of Wrath the Conqueror, which was given to the scribe, Jordyn, daughter of Martinez, who bore witness to the Word of Wrath, and to the testimony of his archangels, who were in the land of Brotherly Love in that day. Blessed are those who read and hear and keep the words of this prophecy branded on their hearts; for the time is at hand.

The Epistles of True Wisdom
The Book of Ancient Future, First Chapter

ONE

EMPYREAN CITY

Heat shimmered off a small airstrip as a glimmering Air Force One began to land, backlit against a blazing sun. The wheels touched down, skidded and taxied to a stop. Within moments, large hangar doors opened, and the regal aircraft was rolled inside.

United States President Joshua Reynolds and a few members of his cabinet stepped out of the plane. They were immediately met by Lilith Morganti, a ghost-skinned brunette shuffling a unique deck of tarot cards. With a visage that was as cold as it was calculating, Lilith greeted the dignitaries with a gloved handshake and a forced smile.

"Thank you for coming, Mr. President. I am Lilith Morganti. On behalf of our staff, I'd like to welcome you to Mount Stronghold."

President Reynolds, a stocky gamecock of a man, dramatically swept his gaze around the hangar at Mount Stronghold, a top-secret location site in Pennsylvania. Usually, the Commander-in-Chief was on point when it came to intelligence and government secrets. That day, though, an oblivious smirk crossed his face.

"What the hell is going on here?" President Reynolds barked, making sure his anxiety was felt by all. "A top-secret meeting in the middle of nowhere while the mutant-terrorists put the world in turmoil... I don't know who this Dorian Von Pyros guy is, but he better not be yanking my chain."

"This is a matter of global significance," Lilith said, seizing a tarot card cold from her deck: "The Lord of Paramount Destiny." "I assure you it will not be a waste of your time."

Lilith headed down a corridor followed by the President and his staff. President Reynolds sidled up beside her, his demeanor less confrontational. "What is this place?"

Lilith stopped in front of two massive security doors. "Mount Stronghold was originally a classified relocation site for civilian and military officials in case of national emergencies," Lilith said. She then peered one-eyed through a retinal scanner on the wall. The doors unlocked with a clunk, revealing an enormous glass elevator. "Now it's much more than that."

Everyone stepped into the elevator and the doors closed. Soothing music played as the elevator descended into an eerie darkness, suddenly becoming jutting stalactites in a low cloud ceiling. Man-made ambient light revealed a sleek, epic expanse of twenty-first century infrastructures that stretched endlessly, suggesting an underground city set under a cerulean-blue sky. The effect was staggering.

"Empyrean City is a utopia for an elite society of Mankind," Lilith said. "We have schools, hospitals, mass transit systems… We even have a lake fed by fresh water from underground springs. It is virtually a self-contained metropolis."

The elevator doors opened and the entourage stepped out. Throngs of residents moved about freely through the perfect seventy-two-degree financial district of Empyrean City. Lilith angled through with practiced ease while the American notables stirred through with a degree of difficulty. No one seemed to notice the President. Nor care.

"Do these people even know who I am?" President Reynolds asked as he teetered from being shouldered past. Lilith nodded off in the distance to a towering statue of a noble gentleman overlooking Empyrean City.

"We have our own government, our own leader, exalted beyond you," Lilith said. "So, you see it's hard for them to be impressed."

The entourage reached an awaiting luxury bus and Lilith motioned them on. As they boarded, President Reynolds focused his attention on a skyscraper with an illuminated display of roving stock market quotations and financial news.

"Commodities?" President Reynolds queried.

"As with any government," Lilith replied, "Trade is very significant to our expansion."

Aboard the bus, the notables stared out the window, their eyes scrutinizing the fascinating subterranean city as it whizzed past. Murmurs rumbled through them as they gazed at the peculiar symbols and statues that seemed to be on every building and billboard, offsetting the splendid cityscape.

"These symbols and images," President Reynolds whispered, almost to himself. "I can't place it, but I know I've seen them before…"

"Our subliminal fingerprints are omnipresent around the globe," Lilith said, "In corporate logos, product brands and in architecture, visible clues as to our sublime power hidden in plain view. And it is here that we, the Brotherhood of the Vampyrians, mastermind and manipulate world events through governments, corporations and the media."

A futuristic aircraft suddenly power-climbed just below the artificial cloud cover. The President looked from the aircraft, to Lilith, to his staff with an arched brow, perplexed. "Why wasn't I told about this?" His staff began to stammer nervously.

"Access to Empyrean City is limited to only a select few from topside, mostly military personnel," Lilith said. "But even the surface dwellers with clearance are not privy to our clandestine affairs. Unfortunately, neither you nor your staff needed to know. Until now."

The bus vanished into a range of trees and wheeled through the gates of Empyrean Stronghold Facility, then parked near the main building which was ultra-contemporary in design boasting perfectly manicured gardens.

Lilith exited the bus with the tour of notables in tow. Everyone stepped back as a group of military candidates ran past in fatigues with the letters "CMTF" stenciled prominently on their shirts.

"This is our base of operations," Lilith said. "After the numerous super-powered uprisings worldwide, Mr. Von Pyros spearheaded a highly-secretive task unit, the Counter Mutant-Terrorism Force, to locate metaphysical agitators and counter the threats."

"So, basically if you want to contest a mutant insurrection," President Reynolds said, "This is the place."

The mood was tense and hushed as Lilith led her party across the huge Counter Mutant-Terrorism Force (CMTF) logo on the lobby's gleaming marble floor. They then went through a glass door, revealing a bustling maze of ceramic tile and glassed-in compounds. Numerous chambers dwelled above and below with tiers married by ramps and glass crosswalks.

"Ladies and gentlemen," Lilith said, "You are now in the last line of defense for the existence of Mankind on earth."

Lilith and her guests traversed a crosswalk and passed a sequence of offices immersed with sophisticated technology. They then arrived at two pressurized doors. Lilith "eye-dentiscanned" and the doors parted --

The place was grand with a ghostly antiseptic air about it. Baroque throne. Gold-leafed walls. Numerous relics from yesteryear. Dozens of the globe's political, religious and social elites were already in attendance, gingerly moving through in awe. Lilith and her entourage filtered into the inner sanctum.

"Welcome to what Mr. Von Pyros calls his 'private realm in the center of the earth'," Lilith said. "He accumulated the world's most precious artifacts from men, who in their quest for power, detached themselves from the magnificence of human life, of which all these wonders represent."

Several bigwigs stopped before an enormous wooden cross that was covered with blood and rotted by the passage of time. The President looked to Lilith, his forehead curiously wrinkled.

"A reproduction," Lilith said with a flushed smile.

An African delegate traced her fingers across the mammoth cross and then turned to Lilith, her eyes beady and suspicious. "What does tour of Empyrean City have to do with cloak and dagger meeting?"

"Everything," a voice echoed. Everyone turned to see an immaculate European gentleman, Dorian Von Pyros, emerge. He looked like he was in his mid-forties but was significantly older. Within the charismatic exterior that could charm a nun or a bum lived a driven individual of considerable power.

"My name is Dorian Von Pyros. Sorry for the dramatics, but the media, even official negotiators must be ignorant to these proceedings."

The Russian President stood heatedly. "Why are we here? Mother Russia does not need to listen to political flunky!"

Von Pyros stepped to him, his eyes cold and cruel. "I have no interest in being a peace ambassador, Mr. Petrov." The

Russian President crumbled under Von Pyros' stare and backed down.

"My only concern is power, just like you. In fact, you are all individuals whose bodies are alive, but are dead of spirit."

The dignitaries looked around, outraged.

"Don't be insulted," Von Pyros grinned. "I can tell instantly with people. That is why you are all here. I'll get right to the point." Von Pyros clasped his hands behind and began to imperially move through them as he spoke.

"History is replete with once-heralded civilizations that were crushed like a cracker in a mighty hand. Egypt. Sparta. The Roman Empire. Assembled here are leaders of nations that are headed for the same eventual fate. But if we unite, combining forces with otherworldly channels, the outcome will be far greater than what can be accomplished alone."

"Otherworldly channels?" President Reynolds queried.

"The supernatural," Von Pyros said. "You've heard of it all of your lives, haven't you?"

"What are you suggesting," Archbishop Gabriel Francis chimed in smartly, "An act of God?"

Everyone chuckled. Von Pyros spun on them, his face flashing like a demon for a split-second. "Not quite."

Their faces went white.

TWO

The Kindred Liberation Army

Six years later inside of Philadelphia's Suburban Station, rush-hour commuters moved herd-like toward the doors of an arriving regional rail train. The crowd instinctively parted as a sinewy black woman, Ashanti Jackson, rushed out of the train with a huge duffel bag clutched in her roughly bandaged hand. Sporting a baseball cap that covered frayed micro-braids, Ashanti was naturally attractive, in a rugged "I'll-kick-your-ass" sort of way.

Grasping firmly onto Ashanti's other hand was her son Masai, an extremely precocious, cute-as-they-come six-year-old. Long haggard locs defined Masai's nomadic reality as he ran/walked, trying to keep pace with his mother as they dashed through the crowd and up the stairs.

Ashanti and Masai emerged into the sweltry Philly sun. Ashanti donned dark sunglasses, magnifying her blood-and-guts presence as she studied the downtown environment closely. The rich, greasy aroma of a fast-food joint wafted from down the street as business suits, tattoos and glamorous faux hair flavored the block like Louisiana gumbo.

A trampled newsletter on the ground. Ashanti picked it up. The masthead read, "Kindred Liberation Times", with the headline, "Detroit Safehouse Raided, KLA Chairman Captured!" Within the copy was a headshot of a severe-featured black man with flowing locs, the byline bearing the name, "Osiris Jackson."

Grim-faced, Ashanti pocketed the newsletter as the sound of wailing police cars neared. She then reached inside of her duffel bag and pulled out a jug of water.

"Here, Masai," Ashanti said, handing the jug to her son, "Replenish yourself with yourself."

Masai obediently hoisted the jug and swigged, blocking his face. As far back as his adolescent mind could remember, bolting through train stations and living unconventionally was normalcy, almost typical. Raised an only child with a steady diet of bouncing around from city to city and staying completely off the grid -- no ID, bank accounts, school or criminal records -- Masai learned early on those upheavals and uncertainty was par for the course in the life of a Kindred Liberation Army revolutionary.

The Kindred Liberation Army, also referred by the acronym KLA, were a radical arm of a class of humans regarded as Kindreds. Falsely labeled as mutants by the media,

Kindreds were people of all races and ethnicities who shared a particular genotype that gave them their extraordinary abilities.

Ashanti lowered her cap as the police cruisers sirened by. She then twisted her cap backwards and fixated on a burgundy car pulling up at the corner. Two hard-looking black men, Aries and Supreme Maffmattixx, stepped out and stood alongside of the hooptie, scanning the block.

Aries, a powerfully built member of the KLA's Philly chapter, hid his watch-adorned wrist behind his back.

"What time is it?" Aries enunciated with proper diction fused with militant timbre. Supreme Maffmattixx took off his shades and looked keenly into the sky.

"Five-forty-three, Daddy-O," Maffmattixx replied, using an endearing urban slang from many moons ago, which he did on occasion. Aries looked down at his wristwatch: Five-forty-three. He formed Maffmattixx an impressed smirk at his uncanny time-calculating ability.

Then with a small jutting flick of the head, Aries indicated Ashanti strolling up to them, Masai close on her hip. She stopped in front of them and removed her shades, brazenly locking eyes with Aries. He broke her gaze with an acknowledging smile, and they then proceeded to perform a dexterous power handshake that could only have come from seasons of camaraderie and revolutionary actions.

"Figured you would've given up trying to read my mind by now," Aries said, clasping a hand on her shoulder with a smidgen of affection, "Especially since you're the one who trained me in psychic defense. It's good to see you, Ashanti."

"Been a long time, Aries," Ashanti said.

"That work you put in at that news show was good shit," Aries said, referring to one of her recent underground exploits. "Took out the TV signal just seconds before those lobbyist devils went on the air. Sweet."

"I decreased the satellite's signal-to-noise ratio, neutralized the human opposition and eliminated those devils before the broadcasters could even cast a glance at the teleprompter," Ashanti said. "Trying to take away our rights with a Kindred Registration Act? I wasn't havin' it."

"Just like back in the day," Aries said as he kindly took the duffle bag from her. He then turned his attention to Masai, ruffling his locs. "What's up, lil' man? You're getting big."

Masai backpedaled behind Ashanti and clung to her leg, regarding Aries with suspicion and contempt the way children do. Aries shrugged it off.

"This here is my man, Supreme Maffmattixx," Aries said as he handed him the duffle bag.

"Peace, Sister," Maffmattixx said as he popped the trunk. Ashanti surveyed Maffmattixx icily as he packed the bag, her resentment directed partly in the way he carried himself, with a certain pride, a cool detachment.

"Don't bother trying to read his mind either," Aries said as Maffmattixx slid in behind the wheel. "You can't."

Off her look that could've frozen Hell, Aries guided her a few feet away.

"Don't sweat it," Aries assured lowly. "Maffmattixx is a mathematical genius and can molecularly shapeshift into anyone and assume their abilities. He's cool, ready to put in work for the Kindred Liberation Army. Trust me."

"I don't trust nobody," Ashanti said coldly, slapping the crumpled newsletter into his hand. "Somebody's giving up tape, telling those devils where our safehouses are, our inner workings. When we find the snitch, I don't want them dealt with until we find out who they're working for, who made contact and how…"

Ashanti's voice trailed from Masai's ears as he slowly meandered away. Bright eyes that concealed a reservoir of intelligence and untapped power stared intently at everything and everyone that passed. They finally settled across the street to a store window with blaring televisions on display.

Since Masai's been born, his parents never owned what they referred to as a "tella-lie-vision" and forbade him to watch one. But to an inquisitive child, that made it that much more enticing. Masai wandered in close, gazing on curiously…

On the TV's, a logo spun into frame accompanied by edgy music. The opening slate for the TV newsmagazine, "The Grapevine", filled the screens. The narrator's impending, monotone voice invited nosy pedestrians to stop and listen.

"Today, on a special edition of "The Grapevine", a radical mutant-terrorist group hell-bent on terror…"

On the screens appeared grainy footage of an auditorium with a hundred or so in attendance, multi-racial with males and females alike. Osiris Jackson loomed over a podium addressing the crowd, his deep voice resonating with militance and conviction.

"We are a powerful family of Kindred revolutionaries!" Osiris exclaimed. *"Undiluted in principle! Solid in cohesion! Sturdy as the root of a mighty tree! Long live Wrath the Conqueror!"* Sweeping his fist aloft, Osiris inspired the crowd to cheer up on their feet with fists raised in the air.

The scene quickly changed to a herculean man sporting a decorated Special Forces uniform and rigid militaristic bearing. His name, "Commander Cassius Monteszuma", slashed across the bottom of the screens as he was being interviewed.

"The Kindred Liberation Army are the most vicious band of mutant extremists the world has ever seen. They have incredible powers with cells operating all over the globe..." Monteszuma's words began to voice-over various cuts:

A beefy Englishman walked into a bank. He de-solidified his body and "phased" through the floor to its underground steel vault. The Englishman then ascended through the pavement outside of the bank with an exorbitant amount of gold bars in his clutches. He hopped into an awaiting car --

On an impoverished Mexican roadway, crowds of people watched as a government motorcade cruised through. A Mexican girl deadlifted a battered automobile and tossed it, barely missing the primary car and members of the scampering Secret Service --

On a war-torn street, an Indian woman hovered above an armored vehicle and beamed a laser out of the Bindi on her forehead, obliterating the tank --

"The KLA executed robberies, assassinated celebrated officials and committed numerous terrorist actions," Monteszuma continued, *"Culminating in the prolonged conflicts we see around the world today, killing untold numbers of civilians."*

The narrator's tense voice returned. *"And its recently captured leader whose outspoken malevolent stance that has provoked worldwide controversy and fear..."*

Masai made his way through the onlookers to the front of the display window just as a snapshot of Osiris appeared on the tubes, his name and mutant-terrorist label scribed underneath. Masai gaped at Osiris with a look of awe and familiarity, studying the similar features they shared; smooth burnt-sienna skin, thick carved eyebrows and wool refined to a crown of locs that framed their distinct handsome faces.

"Osiris Jackson is an ex-war hero, Special Forces," Monteszuma said, appearing back on the screens. *"He went rogue and began teaching military tactics to other mutants."*

An army of some fifty men and women of all ethnicities and diverse physical features appeared on the screens. They stood in military formation, every face intense, every eye riveted forward. Osiris strode in front of them and came to a heel clapping halt.

"Those devils are tryin' to win the opinion of the people, to have an excuse to kill us," Osiris said as he cocked his fist. It suddenly

morphed into a keen-edged telekinetic blade, a ghost-like after-image trailing. *"They don't need no excuse. Come on with it."*

Monteszuma returned in a medium shot. *"Osiris is supposedly one of the few that can actually see "devils" because of his direct lineage to their deity, and his disciples follow him blindly."*

A tall, blue-skinned diva with four arms identified only as "Mutant-terrorist, Kali" appeared, wearing heavy shackles, a bruised eye and a cybernetic halo fitted to her head.

"Our struggle is one of family, one of freedom," Kali imparted with a trained militant-voice inflection. *"To live under the teachings of Osiris is to be free."*

Designated as a religion expert, Archbishop Gabriel Francis appeared fumbling a rosary between his fingers.

"Osiris has never been shy about those whom he calls "devils", who he says work behind the scenes in their bid to control the world. There is no validity to anything he has said, so if anybody is a devil, it's him."

Masai watched the propagandized crucifixion of his father with both pride and dismay. Osiris was the absolute leader of his Kindred brothers and sisters, a shining prince who woke them up from their slumber to the realities of their dormant superpowers and to the demonic arch-enemies they were to do battle against. But on the "tella-lie-vision", Osiris was reduced to an amoeba-like radical who thrived on chaos and vicious hostilities with the global elite. Masai dipped his head slightly as his eyes began to water, but Osiris' stern, paternal eyes bored into him through the TV's, prompting him to pick up his head and hold back the tears...

***

"That's enemy lines Osiris is behind," Aries said to Ashanti. "We could send Masai underground, put together a rescue unit --" Ashanti cut him off hard. "My baby belongs with me and his destiny won't be compromised -- for nobody."

Aries knew she meant it. Ashanti believed her divine purpose was to get rid of the devils that would do harm to her son and she was willing to take that commitment all the way. To the death.

Maffmattixx stuck his head out of the car window and looked around. "Yo... where's the mark bearer?"

Cued by his words, Ashanti's heart palpitated at Olympic speed as she frantically scanned around for her son.

THREE

WRATH THE CONQUEROR

Masai was caught up in the TV's as the narrator voice-overed: *"And the preeminent deity whose teachings their doctrine is built on ..."*

An illustrated depiction of a powerfully built black man with flowing locs hovering above an ancient city appeared, his hands outstretched in glory. The sun flared in his left eye and he had a mark in the center of his chest of a flaring sun with spread wings. His name was **WRATH THE CONQUEROR**.

Archbishop Francis popped back up on the screens. *"The legend of Wrath the Conqueror is that he was a man of the people, who could literally speak things into existence. He taught their ancestors the ancient sciences, the deepest secrets, giving them their extraordinary abilities. He is their Savior, returning in the End-Time to destroy the so-called 'devils' that pervade the world. To us, it's myth. To them, it's reality."*

The controversial intro to the show was barely over when Stanley, a disheveled drunk with a prominent limp, wobbled amongst the small crowd in front of the store window.

"Demons runnin' the world," Stanley chortled, his breath sweet with bourbon, "Bunch of wackjobs. Anybody who believes that malarky is an idiot."

That prompted a pile-on from the few believers present, particularly from Mrs. Ortiz.

"Imagine a world free from war and scarcity, where peace and righteousness prevail," Mrs. Ortiz lamented with a modest Spanish accent. "This is what Wrath the Conqueror will give us. Set this thing straight again."

Stanley jeered. "Have you -- has any of y'all ever seen one of these so-called devils?"

Grumblings circulated through the crowd. Mrs. Ortiz fingered through a painfully worn book with an embossed symbol of a winged sun disk on its cover. It was the KLA's sacred text, "The Epistles of True Wisdom". She quickly found her text and read with the cadence and eloquence of a zealous Bible thumper:

"As it says in the Book of Exponential, the ninth chapter: 'And Wrath the Conqueror smited the devils and cast them back to their wicked domains; that the remaining few will seek refuge in the high temples of the exalted people, spreading their wickedness amongst their inner dwellings until Wrath the Conqueror's return in the End of Days'."

Stanley snorted in ridicule. "So, you believe this Wrath the Conqueror is going to return soon?"

"When Kindred believers start disappearing off the planet in the twinkling of an eye, then you'll believe."

"Oh yeah, lady? When?"

Masai watched the diatribe with pursed lips, his anger churning up inside him. He tried to put his emotions in check, but adolescence overrode his logic. Masai spun to Stanley smugly and the pupil of his left eye suddenly sparked and exploded into a fiery sun with dazzling solar flares a quick second. "What makes you think He ain't already here?"

Some of the onlookers gaped with open mouths. Others backpedaled away. Mrs. Ortiz's spirit promptly boosted as she spread out her arms to Masai as if to a Godly force.

"Wrath the Conqueror has returned! Praise be! Yield yourself to Him for the time is nigh!"

Thunderbolted by a sobering conversion, Stanley reverently fell to his knees. Masai's face flushed with uneasiness as Stanley began kissing his sullied sneakers amid a rapidly growing mob of curious bystanders and inspired supporters. He wished he could take it all back as "Mommy" escaped from his mouth. After all, he was still just a baby.

Ashanti was suddenly there, yanking Masai away. She quickly scuttled him across the street, hopped him into the backseat of the burgundy hooptie and followed behind. With Supreme Maffmattixx in the driver's seat and Aries riding shotgun, the car peeled off.

In the backseat, the air rippled and Ashanti's sunglasses telekinetically lifted from her face and hung in the air. She then spun to Masai severely.

"We've been over this a hundred times, Masai," Ashanti exasperated, her tone scolding. "But Mommy, I was just --"

Ashanti hushed his backtalk with a finger. "You come from a different time, imbued with a unique spirit..." She tugged open the neckline of Masai's shirt, revealing the same identical mark on his chest that the image of Wrath the Conqueror had of the winged sun disk. "And there's a clan out there that will stop at nothing to extinguish your power."

Masai looked at her with pleading eyes. "I want my Daddy." Ashanti eyed him coldly. "Osiris sacrificed himself for us in battle, the way he wanted it."

Masai's lip quivered as he tried to hide how deeply that hurt him. He spun in his seat and stared out the rear window. Atop the City Hall building, the statue of William Penn and the surrounding skyscrapers receded into the background as the scenery began to change dramatically to beer deli's, Chinese take-outs and urban decay everywhere.

Ashanti looked off out the window with a furrowed brow, trying to mask her frustration as she mentally recalled the previous night's events...

FOUR

OSIRIS AND ASHANTI

"Sitting alone in the dark again, huh?" Ashanti asked aloud as she moved into a dimly lit room embellished by the city of Detroit's twilight. As her eyes acclimated to the gloom, she spotted Osiris sitting near an open window overlooking the Motor City skyline.

"No matter where I go, you always find me with your telepathy," Osiris said.

Ashanti flicked on a light switch revealing a neat yet provisional bedroom in an art deco building, the once-beautiful chandelier, ornate columns and stonework crumbling. Ashanti moved in close to Osiris, nestling his head in her bosom.

"I always find you with my heart," Ashanti said, kissing the top of his head.

"Good thing I'm not with my other woman," Osiris said.

"I better not catch you with no other woman," Ashanti said with lethal possessiveness.

"You ain't got nothin' to worry about," Osiris said, hugging her with a great warmth. "Yours is the one and only heart that I'm linked to eternally."

Ashanti blushed in Osiris' embrace, secure that their love was amorous and authentic; united in spirit, forged in revolution. Then her mood shifted to compassion as she rubbed the back of his neck tenderly.

"Dear Heart, you can't continue to carry the weight of the world on your shoulders without proper rest."

Osiris' face flashed a look of seriousness as he looked off out the window.

"I used to have knowledge of their tricknology light years before they made a move on us. Now, somehow those devils get the drop on us before we can even think. They're on their job twenty-four seven. We need to be on ours."

"We have Kindred markings above the doorposts, over thirty sentries holding positions two klicks out and Kali and a half-dozen guards in the building right now," Ashanti said.

"We had more than that in Oakland," Osiris said.

Just then, Kali entered with a bouncing Masai, one of her four sapphire-hued hands holding his.

"How's he doing?" Ashanti asked.

"Masai's progressing very well," Kali said. "His grappling and trapping proficiency has improved immensely, footwork, timing... When he matures and his powers kick in, he's going to be a formidable fighting force."

"Thank you, Kali," Ashanti said. "That'll be all."

Kali dutifully bowed then left. Masai dashed over and leaped into his father's lap, a whirlwind of energy.

"You know you're my little man, right?" Osiris asked, beaming with delight. Masai nodded vigorously and with a dimpled smile, said, "Will I be able to see devils and make telekinetic blades with my hands like you do, Daddy?"

"Greater," Osiris said. "A thousand times greater things you'll be able to do." Osiris reached for a cup of water from the nightstand and poured a single driblet into Masai's hand. "Just as this drop of water has all the qualities of the ocean, there is one power in the universe, and You are that power. Now, show me those katas you've been practicing."

Masai bounded from his father's lap and began performing kung-fu animal patterns with remarkable precision and enthusiasm: Tiger. Crane. Snake. Monkey. Dragon. His parents looked on, smiling sagely.

Ashanti's face suddenly filled with anxiety. She whirled to Osiris with earnest. "Our perimeter's been breached."

Osiris promptly stood and looked out the window, gauging the distance of the sounds of battle. "Take Masai and link up with Aries at the rendezvous spot in Philly," Osiris said, turning back into the room. "I'll hook up with you later."

"What are you gonna do?" Ashanti asked.

Osiris curled a snide grin as his hands morphed into huge blades with a glowing after effect. "You know how much I love a good rumble." Osiris then sailed out of the window on telekinetic winds and soared away.

Ashanti grabbed a stuffed duffle bag and headed toward the door with Masai. She suddenly stopped moving, her features contracting again with a fixed concentration.

"Stay close to me, Masai," Ashanti said. "I can't get a mental lock, but someone else is here."

Masai modulated the speed of his steps, staying tucked close to his mother as she opened the door -- a sudden kick burst blood out of her nose, knocking her to the floor. Stunned, Ashanti scanned around. No one was there.

"Maybe it's a ghost," Masai said, spooked.

Ashanti reeled to her feet. She grabbed Masai's hand and cautiously treaded into the corridor. She turned back often, her wary eyes and psyche searching the shadowy facades as they rounded to a stairwell and descended.

Mother and son arrived on the first floor's graffiti-scrawled lobby. They delicately stepped past several bodies sprawled motionless, Kali among them.

Arriving at the front door, Ashanti turned back curiously as she perceived a sudden psychic shift in the darkness. She reached for the doorknob --

A dagger flew precisely into her hand, pinning her to the door. Ashanti howled as she pulled the blade out of her hand. The door opened -- a punch to the face. She was down again. Ashanti then let off a barrage of psychokinetic bolts in every direction, each powerful blast pulverizing everything into a gazillion dust particles.

Then there was abrupt stillness, except for the feint howls of the wind breathing through the building's many concrete openings. Ashanti scoured through the chalky haze with her physical and psychic senses… Nothing.

Ashanti rose to her feet, her fist clenched and bloody. She clutched Masai close to her with the other hand and hugged the wall, advancing to the exit.

Within the darkness of the wall, an unseen force seized Ashanti abruptly from behind. She writhed and kicked wildly as if she was in some type of lethal stranglehold. Maternal instinct compelled her to telekinetically push Masai across the floor to safety through a deteriorated opening. Ashanti psychically screamed Osiris' name, her strength and consciousness waning…

Suddenly, the wall behind her exploded outward with the force of a wrecking ball, revealing Osiris standing with authority on the outside. Fresh shafts of city lighting now exposed the indistinct figure of Shadowstar clutching Ashanti in a choke hold. Shadows rendered Shadowstar invisible wherever they cast on his body.

With just a wave of his finger, Osiris telekinetically launched Shadowstar into an adjacent building with great force. In his unstoppable trajectory, Shadowstar sailed into the wall of bricks and astonishingly disappeared through its shaded area.

"Where's Masai?" Osiris asked, helping Ashanti to her feet.

"Hiding safely," Ashanti gasped, collecting herself. "I telepathically told him to stay put until I got there."

Osiris slung the duffle bag over his shoulder. "We out."

FIVE

Spinn Doctors

Osiris and Ashanti stepped out of the newly created exit. TV news trucks and pedestrians were stonewalled by local law enforcement as an army of CMTF agents flanked in toward them. Osiris dropped the duffle bag and battle-posed back-to-back with Ashanti like old-school Batman and Robin, his hands morphing again into huge deadly knives.

"Just like our wedding day," Ashanti said.

A CMTF helicopter suddenly came into view overhead, skimming over the situation with its searchlight. Everyone shuffled back as the chopper landed close by. A thick-spectacled Dr. Spinn stepped out of the chopper, followed by his hulking cross-eyed bodyguard, Skizzo.

"Devils?" Ashanti asked.

"No," Osiris replied as he surveyed them, his demon-detecting faculty picking up nothing but mortals. "Just humanity traitors."

"Well, well," Dr. Spinn said with a mocking twinkle, "If it isn't the spook who sat by the door. Hello, Osiris."

"Who the hell are you?" Osiris asked sternly.

"I am Dr. Spinn. I've been sent by my employer to deliver a proposal to you. An interesting spin shall we say, to an otherwise volatile situation."

Osiris reformed his blades back into hands. They would have attacked by now if they wanted them dead.

"Who's your boss and what does he want?"

"Straight, no chaser," Dr. Spinn said as he moved in closer. "I like that. The identity of who I work for is of little consequence at this time but what is important is that he is an individual of great influence and is desirous of your rather effective services."

"What you mean is that your boss wants me to work for him and sell out my Kindred brethren."

"Don't look at it as selling out," Dr. Spinn said. "Look at it as buying in. Your family trinity will obtain riches beyond your imaginations and sit at the heads of all tables. It's a win-win situation."

Osiris' eyes narrowed murderously. "You go tell your boss -- lackey -- there's no way I sell out my people. No way."

With a grunt of hostility, Skizzo split into two, creating a duplicate of himself. The Skizzos lunged formidably in unison, but Dr. Spinn restrained them with a hand signal.

"A broad variety of my employer's interests have been affected by the campaign of terrorism that you have spearheaded over the years..." As Dr. Spinn spoke, Ashanti's face flushed with terror. Osiris read her face, quickly discerning that something was wrong. "But it wasn't until six years ago that you acquired his wholehearted attention."

Ashanti and Osiris looked past Dr. Spinn and saw Masai being hauled roughly out of the darkness by Shadowstar, a blade shoved under his chin. Masai strained against the knife's edge, barely holding down his panic. "Mommy!"

Ashanti instinctively froze, the distress almost making her legs buckle. "Mommy's right here, baby..." Shadowstar threateningly pushed the blade in deeper.

Osiris quickly gestured into telekinetic action. Firearms jerked from CMTF agents' grasps and suspended in the air. They cocked dramatically at Dr. Spinn's skull. "Let him go."

"We don't want to harm the prophetical child," Dr. Spinn said, pushing his weighty glasses up the bridge of his nose. "We're just going to take him with us, hedging our bets."

Suddenly, a soul-rattling wind picked up. Power lines snapped as litter swirled rapidly. Everyone exchanged chilling glances as the ground quaked sharply beneath their feet. People hurriedly backed away as a cragged wave fractured down the middle of the block. Ashanti and Osiris turned to the origin of the cracked asphalt, their look a fusion of astonishment and dread...

Masai was hyperventilating in Shadowstar's clutches at the core of a fierce debris maelstrom, his left eye blazing celestially. Masai shrieked and a burst of psychokinetic power exploded outward from him in all directions. Shadowstar was blown back with tremendous force, tumbling end over end.

Masai's body stiffened with blind rage as the turbulence increased in radius and power, sucking up everything in its path. Vehicles, objects and people became swirling projectiles as they whipped around violently.

Telekinetically shielded and rooted, Ashanti and Osiris watched as their only begotten son vented his terror in an uncontrolled onslaught that could kill a lot of innocent people and quite possibly, level the city.

Ashanti turned to her husband and kissed him deeply. It was one of respect for what he was about to do.

Osiris squinted to Dr. Spinn, who was holding on to a streetlight for dear life. "Let my family go and I'll come quietly. If you don't, it's gonna get real biblical 'round here."

Dr. Spinn scoffed. Suddenly, a decayed chunk of building toppled toward him. Osiris instantly projected a telekinetic field that sheltered Dr. Spinn and frantic pedestrians from the ruin. Dr. Spinn then nodded vigorously in resignation. Convinced, Osiris lumbered through the maelstrom over to a totally immersed Masai.

"Look at me, look at me, 'Sai," Osiris said, grabbing his son by the shoulders. Masai eyed him cryptically. "You are your mind. Master your emotional vibrations."

Disoriented, Masai blinked as the words penetrated somewhere deep in his subconscious, stifling his hysteria. "Now take a deep breath."

29

Masai listlessly took a few breaths, returning to awareness. As his sobs and heaves tapered off, tremors and winds abated. Relief flowed through everybody as they picked themselves up. All around was havoc; wounded bodies, overturned vehicles and brick and mortar ruin.

"You hurt a lot of innocent people, 'Sai," Osiris said. "Coulda killed them."

"I didn't mean to!" Masai cried out.

"That doesn't change the reality, son," Osiris said. "You gotta have jurisdiction over your emotions. You are the One the world has been waiting for."

Masai lowered his head in shame, the surrealistic burden weighing heavily on his adolescent spirit. Osiris picked up Masai's chin with his fingers, locking stern eyes with him.

"Don't ever vent with your powers until you see devils, overstand?" Osiris commanded.

Masai shook his head in acknowledgement just as Ashanti approached, wrapping her arms around her baby boy desperately. She then slanted to Osiris, her heart pounding through her ribcage.

"Dear Heart," Ashanti lamented telepathically, *"I now know that loss of life doesn't always happen at death. The thought of being without you is killing me."*

"Stay strong, baby," Osiris reverberated in Ashanti's mental. *"We talked about this. We knew that this was a possibility."*

Osiris picked up Masai, giving his little boy a kiss on the cheek. Masai half-regarded the affection, unable to keep his eyes off the agents that were looming in apprehensively.

"Can I stay with you, Daddy?"

"Not this time, son," Osiris said with a wink. "I need you to take care of your mother."

Masai's shoulders sagged as tragic understanding flowed into his mental. The father and son bond that was forever was now over. Ashanti took Masai from Osiris' arms and steered him away as famished reporters rushed over, jamming cameras and microphones in their faces.

Ashanti grabbed her duffle bag and gave a last glance back. The embodiment of strength and pure defiance, Osiris raised a power fist to her as Shadowstar, the Skizzos and Dr. Spinn, with a cybernetic halo in his grasp, approached.

"Don't look back to me," Osiris said telepathically, "Ever."

Ashanti then shouldered the bag and briskly pushed through the media circus with Masai in tow. Gesturing, she projected a psychic field of concealment, hiding their presence. People turned away and went about their business as mother and son blended with the foot traffic for several blocks, getting lost in the sea of faces.

"They think with me out of the equation, the Kindred Liberation Army is finished, that you have no power. They're sadly mistaken 'cuz you were always more powerful than me..."

Ashanti and Masai crossed the street and cut through a vacant lot filled with mountains of trash and old tires, racing toward an arriving passenger bus.

"I'm now convinced that there's a fallen angel in our midst. Someone we've trained and trusted has been compromised..."

Ashanti and Masai boarded the bus, taking the empty seats that lined the back.

"But we also have a mole placed on the inside of their secret society. He'll reveal himself to you when the time is right..."

Ashanti wrapped her gashed hand in her shirttail and draped the other around a sobbing Masai.

"Raise Masai up in the way that he should go. Don't let him grow up to be an eagle who thinks he's a chicken."

"I won't, Dear Heart. Until eternity..."

"And then some --"

With that, Osiris was gone, their psychic link severed. A shell-shocked Ashanti looked a-thousand-yards off out the window, a lone tear sliding down her cheek...

***

Back to the future in the hooptie, compassion trumped Ashanti's thoughts as she realized that the emotional distress of Osiris' absence was not exclusively hers. She softened her eyes and whispered in close to Masai.

"Your father was a great warrior, baby, a great man. I miss him, too."

Ashanti looked up and caught Maffmattixx cutting an eye at them in the rear-view mirror. "You got a problem?"

"No, Sister," Maffmattixx replied.

"Is the spot secure?" Ashanti asked sternly.

"The Philly Chapter is representin' in full effect."

"That's what they said in Detroit," Ashanti said. "Oakland before that. Those devils always seem to find us. Make sure it doesn't happen here."

Ashanti's sunglasses coolly slid back on her face.

SIX

HEADIN' UPTOWN

The Uptown Theater, once a world-famous venue for the chitlin' circuit, was now a dilapidated eyesore buried deep in the heart of North Philly. Located on Broad Street, the Uptown was decorated with serious-looking men and women on rooftops and near subway entrances at each corner of the busy intersection.

Torchure, a gothic firebrand, passed out leaflets as he ranted to disinterested passerbys.

"This planet was beautiful once, a long time ago. All this…" Torchure said as he gestured, encompassing everything, "A treasure trove of riches. Various kingdoms flourished. Until the devils came. They hid in the shadows of the highest places, manipulating economics, dumbing down knowledge and controlling information. They kept the earth's consciousness level as low as possible, limiting what we perceive as reality. This became their plantation. We became their slaves."

The burgundy hooptie emerged, pulling up front. Aries and Maffmattixx got out, checking the block. Maffmattixx popped the trunk and grabbed Ashanti's duffle bag.

"All hope was almost lost," Torchure said, "But there was this one righteous dude, born with the sun flaring in his left eye. He taught our people to fight, to beat those bastards back to Hell. He evened the score..."

Torchure's voice faded as he watched Ashanti exit the car, holding the door for Masai. Children frolicked past as he stepped out. Masai's eyes held on them a moment, looking as if he wanted to join them at play. Ashanti tugged him on and headed toward the graffiti-scrawled Uptown.

Torchure regarded them with an inspired look as they passed the inconspicuous totemic markings under the marquee that were used to ward off demons from entering. He then took up his speech with a refreshed passion.

"As prophesied, Wrath the Conqueror has returned and will once again set the example and show us that we too, gotta deal with these devils if we are to call ourselves gods. We can no longer allow their occupying army to come down here and rob and enslave us without suffering grave consequences!"

Inside the Uptown, the auditorium was gutted out, stripped of seats, fixtures and fittings. Hard to believe entertainment juggernauts once performed here. Now it was a revolutionary command center. Cramped sub-normal computer stations were bedecked with topographical maps. A huge printing press spat Kindred newsletters onto a rapidly

34

escalating stack while KLA pressmen bundled and heaved them into carts.

Aries entered the Kindred nerve center, followed by Ashanti, Masai and Maffmattixx. An eerie quiet fell over the spot as tough-looking faces swiveled around to the fresh arrivals' entrance. Ashanti removed her shades and swept a daring glare around.

The crowd parted as Sheer Will the Elder limped forward, his angular hand cradling an ostentatious scepter. Although feeble in bearing, his presence was commanding and respected.

Sheer Will exchanged a revolutionary salutation with Ashanti then moved to Masai. All watched in anticipation as he stroked his whiskered chin, his scepter's "Third Eye" surveying Masai a thoughtful moment. Masai backpedaled slightly behind Ashanti from the critique directed at him. He was nervous but a little excited by it, too.

Sheer Will's face suddenly sparkled as he formed a humbling smile, raising his scepter to the crowd. The place then erupted in pumping-fist ovation and chants of "Wrath the Conqueror" filled the place with a jaunty enthusiasm.

Ashanti grabbed the duffel bag with her telekinesis. It sailed behind her as Sheer Will escorted mother and son through the hyped crowd to a stairwell in the back. Supreme Maffmattixx watched them peculiarly, his eyes never leaving until they were completely out of sight.

"This floor is for the Initiates," Sheer Will said as he bounded the stairs nimbly as a teenager. He reverted to his feeble self as he reached the landing's surface. They stopped and observed a capacity-filled classroom with new recruits settled in behind desks. On the wall was an image of an anatomical man with its weak points designated. On the opposite wall was a blanket-sized poster of the Periodic Table depicting the elements and corresponding chemical symbols.

Ming, a leggy instructor with a sculpted Asian face, stood in the front of the room articulating to her eager students.

"Some Kindreds attain their talents by accident, with no true purpose," Ming said. "Here, in the Kindred Liberation Army, we cultivate our powers through strict discipline and purification, advancing ourselves to a God-like level."

Ming then generated a large portable chalkboard out of thin air. With a materialized piece of chalk, she wrote "Physics of Martial Arts" on the board and underlined it, then turned back to the class. "As KLA Initiates, you must first learn the ancient sciences and mathematics before anything else."

Ming proceeded to scrabble complex equations as Sheer Will strutted off, flagging Ashanti and Masai on.

"A lot of Initiates drop out because of the extensive study," Sheer Will said lowly as they emerged onto the next floor, the air permeated by an overly stifling haze of humidity. "The few brave souls who make it to this level learn to master their passions, liberating their minds and spirits from bodily impediments."

Sheer Will led them down the hall to a candle-lit chamber with the injunction "Know Thyself" prominently painted on the door's glass. Ashanti and Masai peered past the letters and observed a small colony of half-dressed men and women in the lotus position, their sweat-slicked bodies oscillating in a trance-like euphoria.

"They are searching within themselves to find their own unique power," Sheer Will whispered as he brushed away a sheet of perspiration from his face. "Only then can they take the pledge of devotion and study the sacred texts of the Epistles of True Wisdom."

Ashanti gave Sheer Will a smug look, reminding him that he was talking to the KLA chairwoman, not a mere Initiate. He slapped his forehead in "duh" fashion.

"And of course, those who have attained mastery, the Kindreds of Light," Sheer Will said as the trio arrived on the next floor. They bypassed several closed chambers and ascended another set of stairs. Masai threw ping-ponged glances from Sheer Will to the restricted doors as he climbed the steps behind his mother.

"Why didn't we look in those rooms?" Masai thought. With his curiosity piqued and Ashanti's vision obscured by the floating duffel bag, Masai doubled back down the steps.

Masai approached a door and put his ear to it, listening to the thuds and crackling sounds that were coming from behind it. He turned the knob and slowly pushed the door ajar. A teasing glimpse of a flying man shooting energy beams out of his hand was slowly being revealed to him.

Just as he was about to push the door completely open, an unknown force vaulted Masai in the air and placed him down on the stairs. Masai looked up and saw Ashanti standing before him with her hands on her hips, Sheer Will behind her.

"What do you think you're doing?" Ashanti asked sternly.

"Nothin'," Masai nervously replied.

"Get up them steps, boy," she demanded, paddling his butt as he raced up the stairs.

Sheer Will, Ashanti and Masai entered and stood just inside a room. Peeling walls. Piss-like stains on the ceiling. Worse-for-wear mattress. Ashanti turned to Sheer Will incredulously.

"I apologize for the dismal accommodations, but your stay was unexpected," Sheer Will said. "I'll have a team sent up right away to provide you with anything that you need." Sheer Will then exited, closing the door behind him.

"This is it," Ashanti said, dropping the duffel bag, "Where we live. For now."

SEVEN

DAMAGE: CONTROL

In an ultra-hi-tech surveillance room in Empyrean City, three computer geeks, Natasha, Freeloader and Cyber, sat before digital screens that displayed images from the myriad of cameras at the Detroit train station. All heads turned to see Commander Monteszuma as he stalked in.

"Tell me you got something," Monteszuma said.

"We got this from the Detroit train station yesterday," Natasha answered as she navigated a scene that streamed by at twenty times the speed. She then stopped, zoomed in and enhanced the image of a cold and serious-looking Ashanti. "Recognize this woman?"

"Ashanti Jackson, chairwoman of the Kindred Liberation Army," Monteszuma said. "She escaped with her son during the Detroit raid."

Natasha nodded in acknowledgement. "Now peep this."

On the monitor, Ashanti and Masai stood before an ATM machine. Ashanti looked around covertly then touched it. Numerous crisp twenty-dollar bills dispensed out.

"Five hundred dollars," Natasha said, snapping her fingers, "Just like that."

"Wish I had those powers," Freeloader blurted.

Monteszuma shot Freeloader a grave look, displaying his low tolerance for the subversive remark.

"Technopathy," Cyber offered, shifting the attention.

"What?" Monteszuma inquired.

"Aside from psychokinesis, Ashanti is a technopath," Cyber said. "She can manipulate technology and machines."

Natasha broke back in. "Now watch what she does here." On the monitor, Ashanti and Masai stood on an island platform in the train station. Ashanti covertly waved her hand. The monitor's image fizzled out.

"Put our lights out with just a wave," Natasha said. "Two minutes later they're back on and no sign of her or the kid."

"Smart chick," Freeloader said. "Question is, which train did she board?"

The Detroit train schedule popped up and Cyber's fingers tracked down the screen. "Southbound train to Toledo, East to Boston, New York, Philly, West to El Lay... She could be anywhere."

It'll take too much manpower to comb each of those cities and we don't want the local boys involved," Natasha said.

"Undoubtedly, she's en route to a safe house," Freeloader said. "One we're not aware of,"

Monteszuma sneered. "I know who knows where."

***

In an echoing interrogation room, a CMTF guard stood vigil by the door as Osiris sat on one side of a table, the neural-inhibiting halo on his head restricting the use of his powers. A pair of handcuffs conjoined by a straight metal bar manacled his wrists and his feet were double-cuffed.

Although operational torture parameters left Osiris haggard and disheveled, he remained strong and defiant, having been trained by the military to withstand those techniques. But his head lowered slightly as he drifted deep into the caverns of his mind, his spirit sinking with the thought that he may never see Ashanti's lovely face again, and that Masai will have to face his foreshadowing destiny without the guidance of his father.

Osiris picked his head up as Commander Monteszuma and an officer entered. The officer motioned the guard out and slowly crept around the room. Monteszuma removed his jacket and placed it on the back of a chair, regarding Osiris with a look of amazement and dishonor.

"I gotta tell ya," Monteszuma said as he took a seat, "When I heard we finally nabbed the number one mu-terrorist in the world, I couldn't pass on the occasion. How've you been, lieutenant?"

"I'm good, Major," Osiris said. "Murdered any Kindred freedom fighters lately?"

"I prefer to say, 'securing the world against mutant terrorists', but it amounts to the same," Monteszuma said. "Better than killing hundreds of innocent civilians."

"Not civilians," Osiris stated matter-of-factly. "Devils."

"What could possibly make you think they weren't human?" Monteszuma asked sarcastically.

"Real recognize real," Osiris said.

"Two of your victims were Executive Directors of the World Bank," the officer blurted.

"Many are in high places and of great renown, but mysteries are revealed to the meek," Osiris said, quoting scripture.

"Whatever," Monteszuma said with a smirk. "I abandoned that archaic bullshit a long time ago."

"If you can't tell the bull from the shit," Osiris said, "Anything I say will only confuse you."

Monteszuma jeered and went straight to the point. "I'm gonna ask you a simple question and I suggest you answer in a similar fashion. Where's the wife and kid headed?"

Osiris shrugged his shoulders. "You got me."

The officer prodded his finger in Osiris' chest. "Tell us where they went or it's gonna get bloody for your family."

Osiris lunged forward and then jolted back as stinging pains assaulted his brain from the halo. He slumped down in the chair, his dark eyes full of fury. "Fuck you."

In the viewing room, several experts from various military agencies watched the interrogation through a two-way mirror, analyzing every move Osiris made. Skizzo played the background while Lilith shuffled her tarot cards alongside Dr. Spinn, President Reynolds and Archbishop Francis.

"Why didn't you let them kill the little sonofabitch?" President Reynolds said. "Executing their leader's son would have sent a crippling message to those Kindred bastards."

Ear-hustling at the two-way mirror, a balding troll of a man turned into the room. "That would've been a bad idea."

"Was anyone talking to you?" President Reynolds barked.

"This is Dr. Gerald Tucci from research," Dr. Spinn said. "You should listen to what he has to say."

"The compositional elements of the child's DNA is fascinating," Dr. Tucci said. "A sophisticated bio-crystalline energy system that allows him to tune into the total spectrum of energy frequencies in the universe --"

"-- What the hell does that mean?"

"What it means, Reynolds," Lilith said to the President, "Is that Masai Jackson is the prophesied demon slayer, Wrath the Conqueror. His psychokinesis will one day be augmented by the power Cosmic and he'll be limited only by his imagination."

Dr. Tucci jumped back in. "And God help us if they would have awoken his other unearthly talents."

"What are you talking about?" President Reynolds asked.

"I'm talking about physical strength and speed augmentation, energy and matter manipulation on a molecular scale, and a myriad of feats of near infinite levels."

President Reynolds scoffed. "You're delusional."

"Am I?" Tucci said "Then allow me to go from delusional to coo-coo for cocoa puffs. Suppose lying dormant within him right now, that boy could remove the cohesion between cerebral molecules, allowing him to rip an opponent's psyche in two, simultaneously disintegrating their physical form and expending their essence into the atmosphere. Thereby attacking the mind, body and spirit with each strike. And this is combined with remarkable fighting skills that would've made Bruce Lee look like nothing more than a fledgling ballerina. And that is just the tip of the iceberg."

"What do you mean?" President Reynolds asked.

"Suppose he has the capability to turn lead into gold, reform damaged continents and mobilize the masses on a global scale, all from the sheer power of his words."

"He's done it before," Lilith said.

President Reynolds turned toward the interrogation window, his features contracting in momentary disbelief, then cognition. "Does Monteszuma know about this?"

"It's classified, above top secret," Lilith said. "He doesn't need to know."

"What about meds or technical procedures to suppress his powers?" Archbishop Francis queried.

"You think he'll allow us to alter his mind?" Tucci said sarcastically. "Heightened intellect is one of the components that makes him who he is."

President Reynolds' concentration peaked and broke off as he spun back into the room. "What the hell can we do, then, huh? Can't attack the kid, damn sure can't read his mind... We don't even know what he's thinking."

Lilith plucked the "Subliminal Rogue" card. "We'll control the way he thinks."

Dr. Spinn cleaned his aquarium-like glasses as he elaborated on the disorientation techniques that would disable Masai's reasoning. "Imagine altering his behaviors in a subtle yet pervasive way. He can't defend himself if he doesn't know he's under attack."

President Reynolds scoffed. "You're telling me you're going to induce a deity to corrupt himself? Bullshit."

Dr. Spinn put his specs back on. "Projecting situations in his life can have a far greater impact than any physical weapon."

Back in the interrogation room, Monteszuma rolled up his sleeves as he stood. "I seem to remember that you have a heightened threshold for pain. Good."

Osiris raised his cuffed hands, in a "take these off" manner as Monteszuma moved in. "It's more fun this way."

Monteszuma kicked the chair out from under Osiris. He hit the floor. Monteszuma pulled him upright. CRACK! CRACK! To the head. He flung Osiris across the table, sending him rolling to the floor. Monteszuma hoisted him up by the collar. "I want some answers and I want them now."

Just then, the guard returned and whispered to the officer, angling Monteszuma's attention off a second. Capitalizing on the distraction, Osiris swiftly brought his hands up -- WHAM! He caught Monteszuma hard in the chin with the handcuffs' straight metal bar.

Monteszuma reeled back and suddenly began to surge with power from the blow. His shirt ripped as he became larger and more be-muscled.

"Oh yeah, that's the way I like it," Monteszuma growled with a sneer that bordered on perversion. He charged Osiris like a blitzing linebacker, slamming into him with tremendous force. Osiris flew twenty feet to the other side of the room and smacked hard against the two-way mirror, spidering it. Monteszuma's body instantly reverted to normal simultaneously as Osiris hit the floor. The guard exited as the officer meekly approached. "Major?"

"What?" Monteszuma snapped.

The officer spoke to him in a hushed tone. "It seems that Ashanti and her son were seen outside of Philadelphia's Suburban Station."

Monteszuma took a few deep breaths, composing himself. He then picked up Osiris and shoved him into a chair.

"All this time," Osiris said, "You're a Kindred."

"Step out of the dark ages," Monteszuma said as he unrolled his sleeves. "A mutator gene gave me my kinetic-absorbing abilities. While you're waiting to get the chair, pick up a science book."

"You mean a comic book," Osiris retorted.

Monteszuma put his jacket back on, blanketing his ripped shirt as he turned to leave.

"By the way," Osiris called out, "You hit like a bitch." Monteszuma scoffed out with the officer.

EIGHT

NALA BR⊙WN

The room's palate of rich jewel-toned hues and scented candles now expressed Ashanti's concealed softness and innate sense of style. Ashanti and Masai sat meditation-style on an area rug, their chocolate hues glistening with sweat. With a painted depiction of Wrath the Conqueror forming the backdrop, they unwound in deep supplication, releasing the taxing energies of their day.

Masai's eyes blinked open. His gaze veered over to the portable fan in the window, its blades appearing to be slowly rotating counterclockwise. He re-closed his eyes. Fidgeted. Popped them open again. Masai then stared at his hands, his yearning to use his powers white-hot. He first made kung-fu animal formations with his hands and then began to mime the blasting of energy out of them. The slight mimicry then turned into full-scale horseplay, replete with audible sound effects. Ashanti clutched his fingers, settling him.

Masai slipped back into solitude. He glanced at the sovereign image of Wrath the Conqueror, his celestial eye looking down on them protectively. Masai focused on the sun with wings on Wrath's chest, then down at the identical divine mark on his own chest. He looked up at the effigy again, this time with a doubtful expression.

"Mommy, what if I'm not who everybody thinks I am?"

Ashanti's eyes popped open as she turned to him. "Baby, you are exactly who you are supposed to be."

Ashanti motioned him onto the bed. Masai scrambled under the fresh linen, his face flushed with eagerness. Ashanti sat beside him and then began her bedtime ritual of regaling him with a tale of Wrath the Conqueror folklore:

"A Nubian fashioned in the womb by Mother Nature and Father Time... A Master Teacher who lived in harmony with the fundamental laws of the universe... And mighty was he! Blessed with the power to move mountains with his mind and his tongue was as sharp as a double-edged sword that could spit fire... He defeated whole demonic armies... He was taken out of this world by Father Time with the promise of returning him to us in the End of Days... Kindred believers will be caught up in the clouds in the twinkling of an eye... You'll deliver great vengeance to the fiends of darkness, make the land beautiful again..."

Finishing the story, Ashanti tucked him in and kissed his forehead. "Now get some sleep."

Masai snuggled between the covers, his mind filled with imagination and wonder. Ashanti blew out the candles and was about to start out of the room when --

"Can I play outside with the other kids?"

Ashanti stopped in her tracks to this most dreaded question. She always felt a tinge of guilt for isolating Masai from the world, away from his peers. But keeping him with her and his Kindred brethren at all times was the only surefire way she knew to keep him safe from outside interferences.

"No," Ashanti said.

Masai sat up and clicked on the lamp. "Why not?"

"Devils are hunting us, hunting you. You know that."

"I'm tired of hiding," Masai pouted.

"I know, but you got to, baby," Ashanti said sorrowfully.

"It's not fair!" Masai leaped out of the bed, jetted past her and out the door. Ashanti sighed as she regarded a picture of Osiris on the nightstand. "I wish you were here."

Masai shot past a posted guard in the hallway and bolted down the stairs. Ashanti emerged and signaled the pursuing guard back to his post as she went after Masai.

Ashanti appeared on the landing above. She commanded Masai to come back. He kept it moving. Ashanti held up her hand -- he was suddenly still, held by her telekinetic power.

Now here was Wrath the Conqueror, the One whose name was sacred to her Kindred brothers and sisters, the returning demigod sentenced to condemn the Sons of Hell for their iniquities, writhing and squirming in defiance. How could he liberate the world if he himself wasn't free?

After a moment, Ashanti released him. Without missing a beat, Masai took off down the stairs.

"Alright, alright," Ashanti yelled grudgingly. "You win." Masai stopped and looked up at her. "Forreal?"

"You can play outside, but you're still gonna be home-schooled, overstand?"

Masai brightened and raced back. Ashanti scooped him up in her arms with tightened eyes, hoping that her acquiescence wasn't a huge mistake.

***

With a sketchbook propped on his knee, Masai sat on a milkcrate in front of the Uptown building, drawing with meticulous precision. He looked up just as a cute and adorably pudgy girl his age pedaled up on a pink three-speed bike adorned with handlebar tassels and a front basket. Cocoa-complected with neat well-greased plaits, she dismounted and anchored her bike with the kickstand.

"What's your name?" the girl asked with an amicable and feminine confidence beyond her years. Masai looked around. KLA security were situated a discreet distance away in every direction. "Masai. What's yours?"

"Nala." She then reached in her basket and pulled out a deck of cards, amateurishly shuffling them.

"Those your cards?" Masai blurted sheepishly, trying to mask his lack of adolescent social skills.

"They're my dad's," Nala said as several cards cascaded to the ground. "He went away on vacation."

Masai knew that "vacation" euphemism all too well, having seen so many of his Kindred brethren getting hauled off to prison. He helped pick up a few cards, feeling a little more secure now that they shared a common bond. "My dad's on vacation, too."

"I'm staying with my grandmother and Aunt Tee for the summer," Nala said as she pointed to her Aunt Tenisha, a thirty-something faded beauty with a forty ounce of malt liquor entertaining a male duo. Nala then turned back and surveyed the Uptown curiously. "You live here?"

Masai nodded, slightly embarrassed.

"My Aunt Tee says people that live in there got superhero powers," Nala said. "She said it's a secret. Is that true?"

"My dad said a lot of people have powers," Masai said. "They just have to learn how to tap into them."

"Do you have any powers?" Nala asked.

"No," Masai said, re-burying his face in his sketchbook.

"Maybe one day we'll both get some superhero powers... Can I see your picture?"

Masai spun the sketchbook around. It was a drawing of a streamlined car, complete with notes pointing out its features. Masai's artistry and creativity belied his maturity level considerably. Nala was amazed.

"Where'd you learn how to draw like that?" Masai shrugged his shoulders as children rushed over, marveling at his drawing.

"Daaannng!" -- "Look at his drawlin'!" -- "That's decent!" -- "What kinda car is that?"

"It's a solar-powered car!" Masai said spiritedly. "It's pollution-free, got voice-recognition technology, ergonomic air bag system..." Masai's voice trailed off as he scanned their stunned faces. He quickly surmised that inner–city kids his age didn't share the same wide-eyed openness to mature and creative pursuits, so he dumbed it down. "It goes real fast."

"You're weird," a kid said.

"I think he's nice," Nala said with a sweet smile.

"Wanna play with us?" one kid said as he snatched the ball from another and raced off. The rest of the children followed. Nala mounted her bike, waving Masai on. Masai hesitated a moment, then ran happily after his new playmates.

Through window blinds, Ashanti watched Masai, blanketed with a level of concern.

***

Over the next few weeks under the watchful eye of KLA security, Masai subtly conformed to his new environment with ease. He frolicked, played games and rode bikes with Nala and his new friends, his route marked from one corner to the other. They hung out together whenever Masai was not being schooled, which was a great deal of the time.

Aside from scholastics and martial arts training, Masai was tutored in the use of his psychokinetic powers, although he was not allowed to use them publicly. Sheer Will the Elder would hold up cards from a standard ESP deck and conceal them, testing Masai's level of psychic ability. Ming would have him perform rudimentary tasks with his telekinesis, such as turning doorknobs, lacing up his sneakers and pouring cups of tea. Masai quickly excelled in these small areas, fine-tuning his gifts.

Masai also went on long hikes with his mother through Fairmount Park, examining nature's wonders and their functions in the circle of life. On the rooftop of the Uptown, they peered through a telescope and scrutinized the stars and their relationship to events that took place in the tangible world. But their most intense, focused study was on the sacred writings of the Epistles of True Wisdom. Ashanti obsessively drilled him on their hallowed book's genealogies, chapters and verses. He was the prophesied adversary of the devils, and she was making for damn sure that he was not -- could not -- be taken off his square.

***

"See the seven bright stars of the Great Bear?" Masai asked Nala as she peered through the telescope on the Uptown's rooftop. In her scope, the Belt of Orion glittered like jewelry as it prostrated against the autumn night sky. "That's the Big Dipper. The bright star at the end is the North Star."

Off to the side, Aries absently twirled a pair of nunchucks, visibly disgruntled by the subordinate babysitting job. He sputtered under his breath as the children took turns gazing through the lens.

"Ever wonder what it's like in outer space?" Nala asked.

"A vacuum of luminous stars and nebulae," Masai said, lost in the telescope. "Numerous planets and infinite galaxies, a sweet, almost metallic smell..."

"How do you know what space smells like?" Nala asked. Masai stammered, not exactly sure how he knew that. Just then, Ashanti emerged with an unusually cocky stroll.

"Alright, time for your little girlfriend to go home."

"She's not my girlfriend," Masai said. "Just my friend."

"She will be your girlfriend in the future," Ashanti said. "May even be your wife." Both children cringed, Nala's a little less sincere. Ashanti then looked up into the sky. "It's eight forty-seven. Time to get her to her crib."

Aries straightened alert like a deer in the forest, his sixth sense pinched by Ashanti's time-calculating quirk. As Ashanti escorted the children out, Aries' nunchucks astonishingly converted into a rigid staff as he followed behind, studying Ashanti very closely.

***

Fenced in by subnormal high-tech equipment, KLA cyberpunk Maimframe was tweaking the frequency of an outdated computer console, his face kindling electric blue.

"What's the deal, Maimframe?" Ashanti asked as she entered, crossing to him. "What we got?"

"Nothing yet, but those devils are so full of tension, no rhythm," Maimframe said, pointing to the monitor. "See this myriad of blue dots? They indicate the neocortexes of human brains within a two-mile radius. Devils will have red dots. If just one foot of theirs steps in the 'hood, we'll be all over 'em like a bum on a baloney sandwich."

Just then, a KLA soldier rushed in. "We got something."

NINE

SNITCHES GET STITCHES

"Can't move or use your powers, can you, sell out?" Torchure said, an unlit cigarette dangling from his lips. He was sitting backwards in a chair with the handle of a ghostly flaming lasso wrapped in his tight grasp. The other end led to a bloody-nosed Supreme Maffmattixx hogtied to a chair in the middle of a concrete room. KLA faces were all around, craving for blood.

Torchure snapped his fingers and his fingertips sparked on fire. He lit the cigarette, snapped, and the flame went out. He then put the burning end to Maffmattixx's eye, tormenting him.

"Now you're gonna learn why they call me Torchure," he sneered, the words hanging like intimidation itself.

"Listen, I can explain," Maffmattixx pleaded as he craned his head away from the loosey as far as he could.

Aries emerged from the crowd with a backpack. He waved Torchure off, the crowd giving him rapt attention.

"You see, brothers and sisters?" Aries bellowed, "This man is not one of us. Sure, he looks like us. Walks, talks like us. But he is not one of us. You know why, belov-ed?" Aries dumped the contents of the backpack. There were volumes of photos; images of landmarks with peculiar signs and symbols, bigwigs at various functions, but most noticeably, pictures of KLA affiliates. "Because he's an agent!!"

Maffmattixx looked around with grave apprehension at the wrenched Kindred faces. He knew for them that loyalty was treasured and betrayal was a sacrilege for bloodshed.

"I swear, on everything I love --"

Aries bitch-slapped him. "Who you working for, agent?"

"That's not my steelo," Maffmattixx said. "I'm KLA, Harlem chapter. There had been some talk about an age-old satanic order that had resurfaced called the Brotherhood of the Vampyrians. I was chosen to infiltrate."

"Chosen by who?"

Maffmattixx swallowed hard before he answered.

"Kane. Osiris' father."

Everyone exchanged get-the-hell-outta-here expressions.

"Kane studied the stars and concluded that Wrath the Conqueror was going to return in this time," Maffmattixx said. "Knowing I could time-jump a few years at a time, he sent me into the future to get into their secret society on some espionage-type jawn. I was also ordered to look after the mark bearer when he appeared on the scene --"

57

"Bullshit!" Ming exclaimed as she generated a shotgun out of thin air. She then put it to Maffmattixx's temple, chambering a round. "I say treason is grounds for automatic termination!"

Maffmattixx's dark hue sweated pale. Suddenly, Ming's shotgun was mysteriously seized from her hands. It sailed toward the doorway into the hands of Ashanti. All heads straightened up as the KLA chairwoman sauntered through like royalty, followed by Sheer Will the Elder. Ashanti handed Ming her shotgun and stopped in front of Maffmattixx in an authoritative stance.

"What can you tell us about this Brotherhood of the Vampyrians?" Ashanti said.

"It's well-structured with secrets within secrets," Maffmattixx said. "There's an exclusivity of membership; bankers, movie stars, politicians, priests... They are the hidden hand that runs the world."

Aries sifted through the photos, picking up an image of two visibly inebriated geeks at a bar. "Who are these guys?"

"The one on the left is me, perpetratin' as a chemist dude named Henry Murray," Maffmattixx said. "The short bald-headed cat is a scientist named Gerald Tucci. High initiate. One night, Tucci had the raps and went on and on about some top-secret project he's working on. Said the fate of mankind depended on it."

"What kind of project?" Ashanti asked.

"How he's using some jive turkey's DNA to spawn a product," Maffmattixx said.

"A product?" Ming queried.

"It's what he referred to as a clone."

"Who's the product?" Ashanti asked.

"Some big shot. Tucci called him the 'Son of Perdition'." Maffmattixx eyed down at Torchure's flaming binds coiled around him. "Look, I'd feel more comfortable if I was free."

"Me too," Ashanti retorted. "Tell me about the big shot."

Her reply called to Mafmattixx's memory of a black limousine pulling up in front of a deluxe hotel. A valet opened the door and Von Pyros coolly stepped out, the wind ruffling through his designer overcoat...

"He moves through this world with considerable power," Maffmattixx said, "Causing the strongest of men to cower in his presence. But Tucci said that is nothing..."

Inside the hotel's ballroom, a gala fundraiser was taking place. A banner over the stage read: "Embryxx Stem Cell Research Foundation". Von Pyros emerged and sauntered through a sea of commending aristocrats...

"With all the wealth he's accumulated," Maffmattixx said, "All the propaganda he's used to control the masses, all the people he's led to sell out their very nature..."

Von Pyros winked at a stunning Redhead as he took the stage. Lilith handed him a giant-sized check made out to Embryxx Industries for six-hundred million dollars. Von Pyros presented it to a beaming Dr. Tucci...

"He is sheer power personified, hell-bent on continuing the ultimate battle between faith and a hunger for power."

Sheer Will the Elder made a point of studying Maffmattixx very intently with his scepter's "Third Eye". Maffmattixx conveyed back to him complete confidence. Sheer Will knew he told the truth. He then nodded to Ashanti, who signaled Torchure to release him.

"How far up did you move in their secret order?" Ashanti asked as Torchure withdrew the blazing lariat. Sheer Will caught Maffmattixx as he faltered and propped him back up in the chair.

"It took a while, but I finally gained their trust," Maffmattixx said. "Only after a meticulous selection process can you go to the next level…"

In a sacred grove ceremony under the fraudulent Empyrean City stars, mumbled chantings augmented the dusk atmosphere. About fifty people stood obediently, their faces obscured by hoods. Von Pyros sat close-eyed in deep reverie as beautiful concubines, naked under black transparent veils, encircled the Redhead who was tied to a stake, futilely kicking and squirming. A machete suddenly appeared above the Redhead, coming down full force --

"A human blood sacrifice is made," Maffmattixx said, "For you to prove your devotion…

A concubine flicked a long match lighter and set it into a flammable puddle. The pool ignited and coalesced into a huge burning pentagram shape around the lifeless Redhead, illuminating the blood that streamed down her body.

Lilith removed her gloves, exposing aged, withered hands as a concubine gave her an upturned skull filled with blood. Lilith presented it to Von Pyros, who guzzled from it ravenously.

Sensually quenched, Von Pyros gave the skull back to Lilith. She passed it around to the hooded members who drank from it. The skull was then given to Henry Murray...

"I couldn't do it," Maffmattixx said. "I teleported the hell outta there with the quickness. But not before I saw the big shot's face."

Maffmattixx picked up a photo and handed it to Ashanti. It was a picture of himself and Osiris, their hands clasped in a gesture of friendship, with Osiris' father Kane standing behind. Ashanti's face softened slightly against her will.

"That was taken the day before your wedding," Maffmattixx said. "I've traversed so many time streams and periods, to get to the mark bearer in this time, to school him..."

TEN

OPERATION: EMPYREAN SERPENT

"What are they doing over there?" Masai asked Nala as he slowed to a stop on his bike, angling to the vibrant people activity across Broad Street. Nala stopped her bike beside him and shrugged. Masai looked back to where his Kindred guards had been. They weren't there. He then turned to Nala with an inkling of devilment. "Wanna go see?"

Masai didn't wait for her answer. He dismounted and dashed to the corner, flagging her on. Nala wavered a second, then proceeded to follow him across the busy thoroughfare.

Masai and Nala made it to a stoop near the corner where they eyed down from the top steps. A hip-hop head was creating a gritty beat with his mouth as young rappers took turns spitting their rhymes, each one rougher than the next.

Masai watched the cipher, transfixed. Though he noted the urban panache of the emcees, what captivated him most was the intense arrogance and narcissism in their lyrics. Fueled with angst, rage and creativity, the street wordsmiths spoke dynamically of themselves as legendary figures, of antiheroes and gods who could perform wondrous feats. Within their alter-egos embodied the essence of romanticized crime, grime and rhyme. They had absolute power over the elements of the streets and the strength to defeat whole armies.

The rhythm and beat gradually began to communicate to Masai's nature, causing his body to bounce in tune with it. He was feeling it. He looked over at a bopping Nala. She was feeling it, too.

Then, without knowing exactly why, a sudden wave of ill-ease overtook Masai. He slanted upward. Nala followed his look and her jaw dropped...

In the sky about a half-mile away, six CMTF assault helicopters ominously materialized in a formidable triangular formation. At the head of the formation was a larger and sleeker chopper, the Empyrean Serpent. In the stellar aircraft's cockpit, an officer piloted with Monteszuma riding shotgun.

Masai instinctively took Nala's hand and leaped off the steps, taking cover behind the stoop as Kindred sentries moved into positions...

Inside the Uptown command center, six clusters of red and blue blips suddenly manifested and beeped on Maimframe's monitor. His eyes went wide. "Oh shit."

As Maimframe stood, computers and equipment all around began to rip and shred. The fragmented parts assembled into quasi-techno-armor around his body and a cartoonishly-massive blaster hefted in his grasp like an assault rifle. Maimframe clicked a switch on his blaster and a low hum began to reverberate from it...

Outside, dozens of CMTF agents descended from rappelling lines and hit the ground running. Without warning, they opened fire. Armageddon erupted. People screamed, ran and hit the deck. Kindred soldiers rushed out of the Uptown and were met by a bombardment of gunfire. Many were dropped or driven back...

Panic itched inside Ashanti's arteries from the sounds of war outside. "My baby..." She savagely expelled a telekinetic bolt at the wall that exploded outward with the sound of an atom bomb. Ashanti was then out the new exit before the rubble hit the ground, firing lethal psychokinetic bolts at CMTF agents on the move. Kindred bioweapons followed with super-powered savagery, their powerful armaments extensions of their consciousness and skillful bodies:

Aries' body covered with red organic armor as he fell from the sky, landing with the barest impact. He then began bludgeoning into agents with an intense battle lust, his weapon interchanging between sickle, battle axe and spear at will...

Maimframe emerged at the front entrance and was fired upon relentlessly by a handful of agents. He staggered back slightly, the slugs ablating his techno-armor. In his now thermo-digital field of vision, a whizzing alphanumeric readout overlaid the scene, the infrared "devil" figures flashing and "selected"... Maimframe fired his blaster. A missile discharged and splintered into several missiles, precisely blowing away his primary attackers, a rooftop agent and a chopper that crashed and burned blocks away...

Sheer Will the Elder feebly ambled up behind a group of agents firing upon the Uptown. As the agents waved the old man away, Sheer Will quickly saw key areas of their bodies silhouetted blue, their weak spots analyzed and detected... With almost imperceptible speed, Sheer Will took them apart, their bones warping and snapping from each blow...

Ming mechanically pumped out shotgun shells on every agent in her direct line of sight. She quickly discarded her shotty and generated two automatic handguns out of thin air, firing relentlessly on agents in a manic fury...

Torchure took flight and fired fiery bolts at a chopper fast approaching. The chopper exploded and fell out of the sky. Torchure then looked below and hurled fireballs rapidly, engulfing CMTF agents in sustaining flames...

"Just stay here," Masai said as he and Nala huddled in a protective clump behind the stoop, hoping to stay clear of the rounds that patted all around them. "We'll be just fine --"

Suddenly, Masai was snatched up and whisked away by Maffmattixx, leaving Nala frightened and alone. As he was carried off, Masai's eyes met hers with a hint of regret.

With Masai curled in his arms, Maffmattixx's body tripled in height and mass just as a barrage of gunfire rang out from behind. His prodigious frame jerked and twitched violently from the shots hitting his back. Crossing toward the Uptown, he fell to his knees and released Masai, who scrambled back and took cover under a parked car.

With his great strength and will, Maffmattixx staggered up, only to be riddled off his feet again. Bleeding but not mortally wounded, Maffmattixx's body reverted to normal size and teleported away...

In the Empyrean Serpent, Monteszuma and the officer charioted through the air, a hovering Torchure in their scope. Torchure gestured, causing flaming stakes to come up from the ground beneath a handful of agents, piercing through the central mass of their bodies, impaling them.

"Time to let 'em know we're not playing," Monteszuma said. "Take that flying mongrel out."

The Empyrean Serpent flanked Torchure and showered him with a volley of bullets. He toppled and fell a dozen stories.

Masai looked back to the sound of Torchure's body pancaking to the cement. Out of his peripheral, he saw Nala still hunched behind the stoop, the battle royale keeping her frozen in fear. Masai slithered beneath to an adjacent car, crawled from under it and stood upright in front of her.

"I'll protect you," Masai said gallantly, extending his hand. **"Come on."**

Something about Masai's assured tone roused Nala. She took his hand and rose to her feet. Amid an orgy of incessant fire, the child duo made a break for it. They bolted up the steps of a boarded-up storefront. Masai expertly chopped the wood, blasting it apart. They scooted inside and raced past debris and tomcats, beelining their way to the back exit. Masai minced an escape route to the backyard and they then scaled a fence and turned down an alley...

"Target locked," Monteszuma said as he watched a targeting screen of Ashanti giving curt orders and hand signals to a few of her comrades. "Let's bag this bitch."

The Empyrean Serpent loomed overhead, firing on Ashanti. She intuitively whirled and projected an impenetrable telekinetic shield. Dozens of rounds stitched across it. She then held up her hand -- the Empyrean Serpent was frozen in mid-air, held by her power. Another chopper banked hard, coming toward her -- Ashanti hurled the Empyrean Serpent into it. Both choppers crashed and burned to the ground.

The lone figure of Monteszuma loomed out of the burning carnage, the left side of his body on fire. Several agents hurried over and doused him with fire extinguishers...

Masai and Nala emerged from the alley onto the intersecting street. The children hung a hard right and raced to Nala's Aunt Tee, who was standing at the screen door of a speakeasy spot.

"Omigod!" Aunt Tee shrieked, dropping her can of malt liquor. "Get in here, you two!"

The children scampered up the front steps. Aunt Tee scooped up Nala then reached for Masai -- incoming fire drove Aunt Tee back into the vestibule with Masai plummeting to the sidewalk. Nala stretched for him, but Aunt Tee dragged her screaming niece inside and slammed the front door shut, the screen door closing behind.

ELEVEN

KILLING OF THE QUEEN BEE

"Masai!" Ashanti screamed as she caught sight of her child sprawled on the sidewalk. She raced toward him recklessly, drawing enemy fire. A bullet ripped her in the neck from behind, snatching her breath and knocking her forward from the impact. Still on her feet and on the move, Ashanti touched an empty car and the ignition turned on. The car then accelerated and gunned murderously through her attacking gauntlet, smashed into a parked car and exploded on impact.

Ashanti collapsed to the sidewalk, stanching her neck wound. Masai rushed over and wrapped his arms around her, sobbing uncontrollably.

"I'm alright," Ashanti said as she stood confidently, masking her pain. "Everything's going to be okay — "

With a bloodcurdling gasp, Ashanti's chest exploded outward, blood spattering on a horrified Masai. Ashanti peered downward, slack jawed. A blood-soaked spear was impaled through her sternum. She then turned to Masai with a catatonic expression. "Wrath..." Ashanti's body jerked as the spear was yanked out. Masai's pupils became shiny and full as Ashanti slumped to the ground, revealing --

Aries standing behind her, his blood-soaked spear transforming into a flaccid whip. Aries stepped back and watched as Masai instinctively knelt to his hemorrhaging mother, slipping his tiny hand into her lifeless one.

"Mommy, get up," Masai admonished softly as the life-force in her eyes diminished. He looked at the blood pulsing from her chest, hoping that it was only a flesh wound, the kind he heard they get in action movies. But this was real life and Mommy was gone.

"Funeral's over, boy," Aries said as he cracked his whip hard to the pavement, startling Masai to his feet. Aries then moved in, flailing the whip like a zealous overseer.

On impulse, Masai let out a psychokinetic burst that slammed Aries hard into a mailbox. Recalling the vow he made to his father about self-restraint until he saw demons, Masai took off running. Aries recovered and followed him...

With the left side of his body horribly burned, Monteszuma had joined the fracas on Broad Street. Each wallop he received swelled his colossal frame and he released his energy and passions with each sadistic blow he delivered. A battered Maimframe moved in on him, firing bullet-like lasers in rapid-fire succession. Monteszuma charged through, scooped up Maimframe and body-slammed him to death.

"The primary target has been taken out," Dr. Spinn echoed in Monteszuma's earpiece. *"Have your team fire at will."*

"Sir," Monteszuma said, "This is a residential neighbor—"

"—Don't ever question my orders again," Dr. Spinn barked. *"You work under my command, got that?"*

Masai's adrenaline was on turbo boost as he slalomed through cars, racing toward Broad Street. Aries was hot on his ass as he hit the corner and sped toward the subway steps...

An assault chopper suddenly appeared and hovered across from the Uptown. It fired a missile --

KA-BOOM! The Uptown building incinerated. Cars overturned and windows shattered down the thoroughfare as a tower of fire rolled into the sky --

Aries tumbled down the subway steps from the force --

At the far end of the subway platform, Stanley stumbled at a trash can, garbage spilling at his worn loafers. He looked up in time to see Masai teetering through a sparse crowd, falling into him. Masai's blood-flecked hands clung tightly to Stanley as Ashanti's final sounds and horrific image echoed in his head, a tableau that would be in his nightmares forever. "Mommy..."

Stanley was baffled, uncomprehending the reason or the reality. He looked over and saw Aries rising from the bottom of the steps, pressing toward them with malice in his eyes and a studded mace in his hand.

Terrified, Stanley gripped Masai's hand and jumped onto the tracks, disappearing into the darkness of the tunnel.

***

Smoke wafted across the war-torn street. Fire trucks, police cars and the media circus were in full force to see the area where the Uptown once stood sticking out like a missing tooth in a Halloween pumpkin. Von Pyros, Lilith and Dr. Spinn waded through the last flurries of dingy sparks and ash clods of the Uptown. They slowed to a stop as they spotted a horrifically burned Monteszuma sitting on the ground combing through his hair with his fingers. Dr. Spinn leaned in close and spoke softly to Von Pyros.

"A strong military force will be necessary as we establish our off-world interests and galactic power. Monteszuma's unfailing devotion could prove to be quite beneficial."

Von Pyros nodded as they approached, with Lilith studying Monteszuma oddly as he respectfully stood.

"Is pain erotic for you?" Lilith asked.

"Lilith, please," Von Pyros said. "Just count our blessings that we have a kinetic energy-absorbing sadomasochist on our side. Monteszuma and his team took out a slew of mu-terrorists today, before Ashanti got the drop on him."

"That just pissed me off," Monteszuma gloated. "I took out about twenty more after that."

Following Von Pyros' look, Monteszuma spied a metallic-red figure lurking in the shadows. Before he could acknowledge the presence, Von Pyros deflected his attention by clasping him warmly on the shoulder.

"I'll be putting together an elite super-mutant task unit sometime in the future," Von Pyros said, steering him away. "I'd like you to lead the team, if you're interested."

"It would be an honor, sir," Monteszuma said.

"But for right now, go get yourself checked out."

Monteszuma dutifully left. Von Pyros then picked up a half-burnt illustration of Wrath the Conqueror just as Aries emerged from the darkness. "What about the child?"

"He got away," Aries said, his red armor uncovering. Von Pyros crumpled up the picture.

"The child doesn't know the city and he is without Kindred protection," Dr. Spinn said. "When he resurfaces, we will be waiting for him."

***

Masai and Stanley stood outside of a Child Social Services building, both outfitted in timeworn clothing.

"Why can't I stay with you?" Masai asked.

"I know you don't understand this right now, son, but I have…issues," Stanley said, a bitter compassion in his voice. "If you stayed with me, I could foul up your destiny. I couldn't bear to have that on my conscious. Especially not that."

Lilith, posing as a social worker, emerged from the building and headed toward them. Masai looked at her expressionless demeanor then cleaved to Stanley desperately.

"Don't make me go!" Masai cried. "I'll be good, I promise!"

"I know you will," Stanley said as he pried Masai away, maneuvering him toward Lilith. "Miss Morganti is a nice lady. She'll put you with some people that'll take good care of you."

As Lilith led him toward the building, Masai glared back at Stanley with quiet tears flowing from his eyes.

"They're gonna make me think I'm a chicken."

Masai and Lilith disappeared into the building, leaving Stanley confused and destroyed. He pulled out a flask, took a swig then hobbled away.

TWELVE

Skhool Daze

Outside of Cerebralforce Academy in the fairy tale suburbs of Philly, streams of schoolchildren filed through the double doors into the impeccable private school. A silver SUV pulled right up front and parked, an oval "Mathletics Champion on Board" bumper sticker on the rear fender. Inside the vehicle, botoxed suburbanite Meredith Lambert sat behind the wheel taking delicate sips from her hot latte.

Next to her, with a freshly cropped haircut and preppy school uniform, a now nine-year-old Masai stared blankly out of the window. Labeled deficient in attention and obsessively defiant during his three-year chronology in foster care, Masai was shuffled from one foster home to another until a good meaningful couple, the Lamberts, adopted and tried their best to care for him as if he was their own. Although the new copious lifestyle provided more stability, it was much harsher in some ways than the Kindred life he transversed from.

"Why can't I play my video games?" Masai asked.

"Because you are grounded, Mister," Meredith said. "You play them entirely too much anyway."

"Shouldnt'na bought ' em then," Masai muttered softly.

"Probably why you scored so poorly on your achievement test," Meredith said. "You study the stars for fun, know every element on the periodic chart by heart, design some amazing futuristic stuff... How'd you manage to score amongst the lowest in the region?"

"I marked 'C' for all the answers," Masai said as he slouched in his seat. "I hate school."

"Maybe you'd like it better if you applied yourself, Christopher," Meredith said.

Masai breathed in hard as he tried to cap his temper, the new name "Christopher" aggravating his very fiber. It represented to him a total disconnect from his Kindred past and a severing from his prophetic future. He then shot Meredith a hard look in the rear-view mirror.

"Why'd you give me that ol' dumb name anyway?"

"What's wrong with it?" Meredith asked with an upbeat tone. "Christopher is a good name."

"I like my old name better." Masai unhooked his safety belt, exited the vehicle and slung his backpack over his shoulder. He tugged his straight-legged khakis down a little then walked toward the school.

"Christopher!" Meredith yelled. Masai hesitantly about-faced. "I know having a new family is tough, on all of us... When you come home, I'll make those smothered pork chops and onions you love so much, okay?"

Masai beamed with fresh enthusiasm and rushed toward the school where a few of his classmates were huddled together by the front steps. One of them was Nala, her chubby face alive and fresh as a sunflower.

After her surrealistically traumatic summer in North Philly, Nala moved back into her suburban neighborhood with her parents, her father having been released from prison a year later. To Masai and Nala's delight, they happened to live in the same community.

In their affluent stomping ground, Masai and Nala grew very close. Masai spat his rhymes for her and shared his innovative designs and ideas for a cybernetic city system that centered on energy efficiency and advanced automations. Nala listened, not really understanding any of it, but relished the joy and energy that shined in his eyes whenever he talked about it. Masai marveled when she performed her card tricks and listened attentively to her innermost secrets. Without saying so, they had become best friends, and each was as sure about that as if it had been spoken. At no time did they talk about what happened on that fateful day on Broad Street. They both understood that it was a sore spot in both of their lives, especially Masai's, so they kept the topic off-limits.

***

Masai sat in the back of the class, his cheek resting on the desk while defacing it with graffiti. He was bored. Tired. Pissed.

Masai's gaze slid over to Nala who was seated across from him. Her chunky legs were curled around the chair's limbs, and she had a book standing on its end, blocking the front view of what she was doing behind it.

Masai sat up and watched as Nala gestured, agitating the air molecules. Gaseous winds swirled as she generated a snowball out of thin air, bringing to light her powers of ice.

Nala secretly toyed with the snowball, tossing it lightly into the air. With gradual boldness, she lobbed it a little higher, sailing the snowball slightly out of reach. She stretched and caught it. Masai met her eye to eye. Busted. Nala turned away sheepishly and dissipated the snowball into the atmosphere.

Masai was surprised and elated to know that she was a Kindred. He quickly scribbled on a piece of paper and folded it. He tapped Nala and handed her the note. She fanned the paper out and read it:

"Do you want to go with me? Check box YES or NO."

Nala beamed and checked "YES". She re-folded the paper and handed it back -- Mr. Watson was suddenly there, snatching it.

"I'll be sure to inform your parents of your courting methods during class time," Mr. Watson said, balling up the note. Nala tried to hide her shame, but her tears told the story.

"Give it back," Masai demanded as he stood assertively.

"I'd advise you to sit back down and do squat like you've been doing all year," Mr. Watson said daringly.

"Not until you give it back," Masai said.

"It's little degenerates like you that bring down the good students," Mr. Watson said. "Well, not on my watch."

Masai snatched the balled-up paper out of his hand. Mr. Watson forcibly gripped his arm. "You're going to the Principal, Mister." Masai expertly countered and seized his wrist, applying pressure. Mr. Watson sunk to his knees, barely stifling a scream.

Masai let him go and looked around. The class was completely frozen on him. His eyes found Nala. She formed him a cherished smile. Masai then turned and hoofed out. Dizzied, Mr. Watson crawled to his feet as a wave of snickering enshrouded the class.

***

Principal Pederson eyed down at the schoolyard where Masai was freestyle battling against another student with a buoyant school audience looking on. Behind the Principal, Meredith Lambert and Mr. Watson were seated with Lilith.

"I'm sorry, Mrs. Lambert," Principal Pederson said, turning into the room. "Christopher just doesn't seem to fit in here. Low test scores, lack of participation --"

"Repeated aggressive behavior," Mr. Watson interjected. "The child loves to fight and he's remarkable at it."

"Fortunately, his assaults are never with peers," Pederson said. "Just less-favored teachers and older bullies."

"And anyone who messes with Nala Brown."

"Although noble, totally unacceptable," Pederson said.

"For god sakes," Meredith implored as she slapped down a handful of Masai's drawings in front of the principal. "He's bright, brighter than any child I've ever --"

Lilith cut her off. "We just feel Christopher should be somewhere that can accommodate his…special needs."

***

In an over-filled remedial class, Masai sat in the back, numb and withdrawn. He felt as if he was stuck in some type of netherworld as he watched students, a few with obvious physical and mental afflictions, engage in juvenile revelry. The teacher, Mrs. Ferguson, disregarded the chaos as she sat at her desk reading a newspaper.

The jarring thump of rap music going by. Masai's frown drifted out of the window toward it, past the schoolyard and over to the row homes where a vagabond was roaming through discarded items and rubbish. Upon closer inspection, Masai realized that it was Stanley.

Masai arched his back straight as his eyes danced back and forth from Stanley to the anarchy of the class. A decision made, he grabbed his belongings and took a determined stride to the front of the room. Mrs. Ferguson looked up from her paper. "Where do you think you're going?"

Masai said nothing as he scanned her paper's headline: "KLA Falls Apart After Loss of Key Leaders, Internal Splits." Sickened, he traipsed out the door.

"I hate it when they don't take their meds," Mrs. Ferguson mumbled to herself.

Masai moved quickly down the hall. Mrs. Ferguson emerged from the classroom in hot pursuit.

"Christopher, get back here!"

Masai's pace accelerated. He turned a corner and bolted down the steps, through the doors, out of the schoolyard, onto the street and into the ghetto forever.

THIRTEEN

GROWTH BLUNTING MENTALITY

Bells jingled as a broad-shouldered figure sporting an obscuring hood came through the door of a neighborhood convenience store. Mrs. Ortiz, tending to customers at the counter, looked up occasionally as the mysterious figure hitched up his sagging jeans and moved through to the back of the bodega with the raw passion and enigma of a street thug. He stood before an ATM machine. Touched it. Several crisp twenties spat out.

After grabbing a hearty handful of junk food, the mystery man approached the counter and stacked the munchies on top of it. He then removed his hood, revealing a mane of locs that framed his familiar handsome face and magnetic eyes which were now older, harder and colder.

"Hola, Masai," Mrs. Ortiz greeted with a warm smile.

"'Sup, Miss Ortiz. Let me get a Vanilla Dutch," a jaded twenty-two-year-old Masai requested with streetwise timbre, referring to the flavored cigar used to roll a blunt.

"Strong spirits are the enemy of the mark bearer," Mrs. Ortiz said as she bagged the items, "For they will hinder his divine gifts which can only cultivate by their hunger to exist. The Book of Tribulations, chapter three, verse seven."

"No one can covet the mark bearer's journey," Masai retorted as he paid, "For his life alone must be his teacher and disciple, in order to comprehend the Book that is Himself. Innerstanding, chapter twelve, verse eighteen." Mrs. Ortiz smiled as Masai grabbed the bag and exited.

Under the North Philly canopy of darkness and snow flurries, Masai pulled up his hood and trekked up the street.

"'Sup, Miss Johnson," Masai said to a middle-aged woman shoveling snow in front of her home. He took the shovel from her and began scooping up snow and dumping it at the curb. "Ehrrything good?"

"Just fine now," Mrs. Johnson said, "After you showed those young punks a lesson."

"You got any more problems, let me know," Masai said, dumping the last pile. "I can't wait to act a fool again."

Masai gave her shovel back and moved on from her smile. He exchanged a covert swap with a hustler and then headed to a boarded-up building. Wires led from the dwelling to a streetlight which allowed resident squatters to jack the power. Masai hitched up his sagging jeans, passed under the Kindred markings above the door and went inside.

In a darkened living room, TV illumination varnished across Stanley who was passed out on a couch. On the TV, reporter Jordyn Martinez was speaking with professional journalistic decorum.

"Since the collapse of the Kindred Liberation Army more than a decade ago, copycat mutant-extremist groups have been popping up all over the place," Jordyn said as the scene switched to a group of quasi-religious disciples, their faces and hearts facing the heavens. *"One such group, the "Hands of Wrath", functions as a network comprised of both a mutant army and a Wrathism movement that calls for strict interpretation of Kindred doctrine..."*

A key married a lock and Masai entered, turning on a light. The place was shabby, furnished mostly with stuff others threw away. Except for the empty beer bottles that cordoned Stanley off like orange pylons at a construction site, the place was relatively neat.

Masai peeled off the hoodie from his lean muscular frame and tossed it on a chair. He then gave a glance at the TV where Hands of Wrath leader Johann Faust, with atomic energy flaring around his hands, was sneering back at him.

"The Kindred Liberation Army was targeted for annihilation because they were the brightest beacons for freedom in the world," Faust said with a menacing fanatical tone. *"That is why we, the Hands of Wrath, will intensify that light, by making their demonic system buckle under the burden of our attacks --"*

Masai turned off the TV. He was so far removed from his esoteric upbringing and was satisfied to exist in the growth-stunting mentality of the 'hood. The way he saw it, the less he knew, the better. Broadening his worldview might force him to have to be accountable, a change he wasn't willing to make.

Masai then turned his attention toward Stanley, who was changing position in his slumber. Ever since he ran away, Masai had been very grateful to Stanley for taking him in after much prodding. Stanley didn't want to take care of anybody or anything, not even himself. But his compassion for Masai, coupled with a spiritual void he wanted to fill within himself, annulled his indifference. Now Masai was numb with the thought of how Stanley's alcoholic abuse solidified the guilty judgments of his mind and his body and soul were now carrying out the sentencing. Masai discarded the beer bottles and went upstairs.

Masai entered his bedroom. Designs of advanced modes of transportation and home dwellings were situated on the walls and a telescope existed on top of a bookshelf, the only visual representations of a life long forgotten. Masai made his way over to a mirror, his assessments of Stanley and his own reflection now staring back at him.

"There's one power in the universe and you are that power," Masai affirmed aloud to himself. He then scoffed, flagged his reflection and moved away.

Masai clicked on head-knocking rap music, convened at a table and fished in his bag. He pulled out a cigar and placed a small bag of marijuana on the table. He stared intently at the cigar, flexing his mind. The air rippled as the cigar's packaging began to unwrap and the cigar cracked itself open. It amazingly gutted itself of tobacco and the weed sprinkled in, devoid of seeds. Masai picked it up and lick-rolled himself a phat blunt. He then lit it, leaned back and toked.

***

Beneath a streetlight, the members of the Get Dat Gwap Clique, Punchlyne, Khansepp and Nikki Swagg spat their rhymes into the cold air amid a bouncing crowd. The fourth and final member, Masai, stepped forward with inherent charisma, alpha-male gait and a blunt in his hand. He was now his rap alter-ego, Wrath Da Spitacular, his voice an amalgamation of poet and thug with the weight of a preacher. Masai's street testimony coursed through them with a pious frenzy as they oohed and aahed from his clever metaphors and punchlines that flowed like fluid.

"Yo, Wrath," supple gangstress Nikki Swagg said as she looked up the street, cutting off his flow, "Ain't that your Ol' head?" Masai shuffled up a bit to get a better look...

At the other end of the block, a noted group of young hellions, the York Street Jackers, were pummeling Stanley against a wall. The Jackers were notorious for dispensing havoc in the community without provocation. That day though, was Judgment Day.

"Hit him again, Lil' Mook," yelled Tyrone, the rangy leader of the Jackers. He and his goons watched as Lil' Mook punched Stanley in the head, knocking him off balance.

"Let me show you how it's done, son," Tyrone said as he moved in, striking Stanley hard. Stanley toppled backwards,

85

his leg twisting awkwardly under him as he sloshed to a blanket of snow. He then curled in the fetal position and covered his head to cushion the blows to come.

"He won't be out here begging no more," Tyrone said as he landed a kick to Stanley's mid-section.

Suddenly, Tyrone was yanked away and slung hard to the pavement. All heads suddenly focused on the figure of Masai standing there between them and Stanley. The Jackers exchanged hesitant looks. Masai glared at them fearlessly, reading the odds with delight.

"Who the fuck is you?" Lil' Mook said, a hint of sudden bitch in his voice. Masai answered with a kick to Tyrone's face. The Jackers then moved in ominously, attacking all at once...

Masai tore into them, his movements agile and precise, his attack, swift and vicious. In a series of stunning moves, noses exploded blood, limbs were snapped, and balls were bashed into guts.

Lil' Mook arched a gun. In a move almost too quick to see, Masai parried, seizing his wrist. The gun went off, missing by inches -- it dropped as Masai unleashed a devastating combination that ended with Lil' Mook's head smashing through a car window.

It was over in a flash. About a dozen Jackers were laid out, beaten and bloodied. The rest of the Get Dat Gwap Clique rushed up and pelted on the finishing touches.

Tyrone crawled through the snow towards the gun a few feet away. Masai stepped in front of him and picked it up. In a single one-handed move, he disassembled the gun.

"He's a bum...always out here begging and shit," Tyrone whimpered as he looked up and saw the figure of Masai silhouetted apocalyptically against the streetlight, the sun flaring in his left eye. For a moment, he resembled the avenging deity that he was prophesied to be.

"W-What...who are you?" Tyrone said, chilled to the bone. Masai gripped up Tyrone hard and jabbed his thumb into a nerve cluster in his neck. "Please... don't do this," Tyrone beseeched in a constricted mutter.

"Who's begging now?" Masai said, his eyes trembling in cold fury as he pressed his thumb in deeper. Spectators began to assemble, pleading with shrills of mercy on Tyrone's behalf.

Out of his peripheral, Masai noticed an enigmatic figure standing near the far end of the gathering. Streetlights danced off the jewels that decorated his leather jacket. Although Masai didn't recognize him, his presence felt strangely familiar, a Kindred soul reminding him of a forgotten heritage.

Masai's eyes flickered a thoughtful moment. He then looked over fully to where the mystery man was standing. He was gone.

"This will put you on the grid, son," Stanley said as he wobbled in close to Masai, watching as Tyrone's eyes rolled up in his head, "And we both know that's not where you need to be right now."

Heeding Stanley's wisdom, Masai let Tyrone go, collapsing him in a patch of snow like a sack of potatoes. He then released a pent-up breath and stood over him imposingly.

"Don't throw stones at people for a standard you can't uphold yourself." Masai then turned to Stanley. "You ah-ight?"

"Always," Stanley said, a rivulet of blood running down his chin. "Long as I got a God on my side."

***

With his locs wound up in a bandana, Masai scrambled eggs at a hot plate in a make-shift kitchen. Stanley hobbled in, sat down and took a strip of bacon from a dish on the table.

"That was some fireworks yesterday," Stanley said, munching on the crisp swine. Masai said nothing as he doled out the eggs. "So what are you gonna do?"

"Get signed," Masai said as he took a seat. "Make Wrath the Spitacular a household name. Get that paper."

"No, I mean about fulfilling your destiny. Being the Savior to the world," Stanley clarified.

"I don't believe that shit no more," Masai said, taking in a mouthful of eggs.

"I don't believe that," Stanley said, "And you don't either."

"What do you expect me to do?"

"Be what you were sent here to be," Stanley said.

Masai grabbed his hoodie from the back of the chair and headed out to leave.

"Nobody can see them, you know," Stanley said.

"See what?" Masai queried.

"The chains," Stanley said, "Enslaving your mind."

Masai turned back and tossed a wad of cash on the table. "I'm not the only one around here wearing shackles." Masai strode out and slammed the door.

***

Masai puffed on an "L" behind the wheel of his hooptie, his mental sky darkened by a cloud of guilt. During their time together, Stanley protected him, borrowed and stole to feed and clothe him. He felt the least he could have done was give his O-G a little more respect.

Masai navigated through a strip mall where the other members of his crew were hustling their bootleg rap CD's in front of a liquor store. Seeing Masai's car, the group moseyed over and climbed in. The car then pulled off and headed down the avenue.

Riding shotgun, Nikki Swagg affectionately began to play with Masai's locs as he drove. Annoyed, he flicked her hand away. Even though they were occasional "smutty buddies", he wasn't feeling her the way she was feeling him. Nikki sighed and reached for his blunt.

"I'm sick of hustlin' our CD's on the street," Nikki said in-between tokes. "We need to post up at a spot where ballers and producers be at."

"I found one," Khansepp said. "A club down the way."

"Ain't no club down the way," Nikki said.

"Just opened up a coupla weeks ago," Khansepp said. "It's called Club Kindred, where the old Uptown was at."

Masai cringed, a sinking feeling in his gut. Even though he lived close and knew it existed, he avoided the area like the plague, in no rush to be reminded of his memories of unspeakable horror.

"Major label heads be parlayin' there searching for new talent," Punchlyne chimed in, passing the weed. "My homie's the deejay and hosts a new jack set on Saturdays. He'll get us in and we can perform our shit. Then it'll be on and poppin'."

"Ain't that club named after those crazy mutant-terrorist dudes that used to be in there?" Nikki asked.

Masai's molars clenched as they went on a seemingly endless castigation of the Kindred Liberation Army:

"They had powers or some shit..." –

"Heard they killed a lotta ma-fuckas..." –

"Their God told them to do it..." –

"They was prolly smokin' some of this shit right here..."

That's it. Masai braked, stopping right in the middle of the street. He spun on them severely, his voice machete-like.

"The Kindred Liberation Army was about the people, about freeing the minds of deaf and dumb muthafuckas like y'all! They had a kill-kill equation! They only killed for the same reason they were willing to die! And they'd rather die in the struggle than live under the stagnated insanity of this demonic world! What are y'all pussies willing to die for, huh?"

Masai resumed driving as they traveled several blocks in awkward silence. After a noiseless round of puff-puff-pass, Nikki broke the quiet. "I say we go check it out. Is you wit' it?"

Masai didn't answer, lost in himself.

FOURTEEN

CLUB KINDRED

Opulent cars crammed parking spots on both sides of Broad Street as young players and scantily clad women anticipated entry into the swank Club Kindred, a pentagram shape subtly hidden in its glowing logo.

Punchlyne rounded the corner onto Broad Street, followed by Khansepp, Nikki Swagg, and Wrath Da Spitacular. Dressed urban designer-chic, the half-baked Get Dat Gwap Clique strolled coolly toward the nightclub.

Masai, with his precise locs pulled back revealing a diamond earring, lagged back and stared at the nightclub in apprehension. After a moment, he followed them.

Punchlyne performed a hard mechanical knock on a steel side door with thumping music coming from behind it. A speakeasy slot slid open, revealing a pair of eyes. The door unclosed and Punchlyne gave the burly doorman a pound, entering. The rest of the crew followed him in.

The Kindred nightclub was euphoric to the carnal senses, replete with ballers, trendy libations and phat ghetto ballerinas in cages. A huge monitor wall displayed an array of music videos as partygoers swayed to the bone-quaking bass of the latest jams.

Masai followed his crew deep into the belly of the packed crowd, exchanging "what's up" nods, pounds and hugs along the way. As Masai turned from an embrace, a stray hand reached out in front of him to tap a curvy vixen, severing him from his crew. The vixen scoffed past, ignoring the touch. Masai turned to the owner of the hand, a preppy college kid.

"Stuck-up bitch," Masai heard College Boy say, but when he spoke, his mouth didn't move. College Boy then turned to Masai and without moving his mouth, said, *"What are you looking at?"*

College Boy turned and walked away. Masai reeled as he realized that he heard the voice inside of his own head.

"Fuck out the way, homie," A burly hustler mentally said as he rolled up with his gangsta-scowl on, leading his crew. Responding to the hustler's thoughts, Masai atypically moved aside and allowed the hustler train to cruise by.

Gradually, a cacophony of foreign thoughts, secrets and inclinations began to bombard Masai's inner world. Dizzied, he threaded through the deluge of people to a spot at the bar near the pool table. He then began self-consciously performing paranoid weed-checks of his appearance.

In the VIP area that overlooked the dance floor, a ripened Nala cradled a champagne flute as she held court with three admiring power players. The beauty beneath her gorgeous face and brown sugary skin shined through as it always did, but now her finesse was expressed by natural tresses, graceful movements and chic apparel that showcased her thick Jessica Rabbittesque body. Her girlfriends, Axiss and Emosha, meandered over just as the baller trio walked off, seemingly gratefully dejected.

"Those guys were so corny," Nala said. "The one with the grill in his mouth said he played pro football for the Eagles. Like that's supposed to impress me."

"Where'd he go, girl?" asked Axiss, a petite diva garbed in a tight mini-dress and impeccable hair-weave. "He's the one with that paper."

Emosha, a pony-tailed hellcat whose lethal demeanor overshadowed her beautiful Asian features, gave Axiss the gas face. "And you wonder why you can't keep a man."

Axiss twisted her lips and looked off, her eyes anxiously flitting over the designer clothes and jewelry of the ballers in the club. She finally settled them down at the pool table area.

"Hoodrat is such a freak," Axiss said. Nala and Emosha followed her look…

Hoodrat, a ratchet chick who was all tits, tats and ass-crack, vyed for attention by bending over the pool table with her butt purposely thrusted out as she lined up her shot.

Surprise flared in Nala's eyes as she checked out the guy seated at the bar behind Hoodrat. It was Masai.

Nala was breathless, her senses pleased. Emosha noticed the change that came over her.

"You still care for him very much,". Emosha said.

"Girl, you already know how I feel," Nala said.

"I don't know what you see in him," Axiss said, trying to knock Nala down a notch on the low. A self-assured Nala brushed off the remark. She had the goods, knew it and walked comfortably and confidently in her own light. Emosha didn't have such empathy as she cut Axiss a cold look.

"What?" Axiss responded. "I'm just sayin'. He don't look like he got no money."

"To you he might be a plain ol' rock," Emosha said, "But to her he's an uncut diamond."

"Well, just like the rest of the rocks do, he'll leave her. Brokenhearted and stone-broke." Nala pointedly moved away.

***

Masai was giving Hoodrat's exposed ass-crack the once over as an enticing fragrance suddenly breezed in his nostrils accompanied by a sweet voice. "You don't want that, do you?"

Masai turned and saw Nala sitting on the neighboring stool, her shapely legs crossed and hands resting demurely in her lap. Her beauty astonished him as his eyes suddenly sparkled in suspended time, leaving behind his inhibitions.

"Hell no," Masai said.

"Better not," Nala imparted lightly. They then hugged with a familiar chemistry.

Sulking with envy, Hoodrat tossed her cue stick across the pool table and stormed away.

"Look at you," Nala said, "All thugged-out now."

"Look at you," Masai said, "Lookin' all scrumptious."

Nala blushed with a soft but incandescent smile.

"So wassup witchu?" Masai asked as he commanded the bartender with two fingers, indicating drinks. "Whatchu doin' back down here?"

"I was hoping to run into you," Nala said. Feeling it was a little too presumptuous, she played it off. "Seriously, I'm just hanging out with some colleagues, celebrating."

"What's the occasion?" Masai asked.

"Our last weekend above ground," she replied.

Masai tilted his head quizzically. "Don't tell me you're involved with some crazy death cult."

"No, silly," Nala said, giving him a "love tap" on the arm. "I'm in a secret unit, the Omega Squadron. We'll be living underground in a sort of military compound."

"For what?" Masai queried.

"It's classified, but I'll tell you this," Nala said as she produced a playing card. It froze in her grasp, icicle-etched so sharp it could dissect a rock. "It's for those of us with special abilities. We've got our own call signs and everything."

"What's your call sign?" Masai asked as the bartender returned with drinks. "Glacia."

Nala, now referred to as GLACIA, leaned in close and switched into gossip mode.

"See the short stocky guy?" Glacia said as she discreetly pointed up at the VIP section to a youthful Italian street-tough built like a pint-sized Mike Tyson. "That's Kid Hardkore. He's freakishly strong and will mix it up with anybody... I think he's got a crush on me."

Kid Hardkore sat with his brawny arms crossed, totally disinterested in the big-boned Cougar who was seemingly telling him her whole life story.

"He's best buds with Johnny Fatal," Glacia said regarding Johnny Fatal, a Hispanic playboy whose hands and face were bluish green with tattoos. Johnny Fatal mischievously nudged Hardkore with an elbow. Hardkore elbowed him back. "He's a living tattoo."

Just then, Axiss marched up to Glacia, her face twisted in disgust. "Now I see why you don't hang with Hoodrat no more. She's a straight-up hoe. She's having sex with some guy in the bathroom just that fast. She don't even know him."

"Told you," Glacia said. "And you're lucky. It's only one guy this time." Axiss walked off, shaking her head in disgust.

"Who's that jawn?" Masai asked.

"That's Axiss," Glacia said. "She absorbs power from the sun and can generate solar axes. She was talking about Hoodrat, the one whose butt you were checking out. She runs after men like there's a penis famine on the planet..." Glacia took a breath, catching herself. "Don't get me started."

"I wasn't checking out her butt," Masai said.

"Anyway," Glacia said, redirecting his attention back to the VIP section, "The one with the ponytails is my girl Emosha.

96

She's an empath with photon powers and ninja skills. The girl is vicious."

Glacia and Masai watched as Emosha stared daggers into an approaching Casanova. He kept it moving.

"The heavy-set guy is Kataklysmo," Glacia said, indicating a potbellied barbarian guzzling beer straight out of a pitcher. "He can make his body explode and reassemble. Now he's the bomb... There's a couple more of us sprinkled around here somewhere..." Glacia then turned her spotlight back to Masai. "So what have you been up to? Putting those natural resource-based designs to good use, I hope."

"Just chillin'," Masai said, "Doin' the rap thing."

A strange look of skepticism and disappointment crossed Glacia's face momentarily. She then changed the subject.

"Remember when we were kids... What was the first name you had as an emcee?" Masai chuckled, then spelled out the letters. "H-I-M. His Imperial Majesty."

"Oh yeah," Glacia said, beaming in retrospect. "I remember you had your video all planned out. Your face would always be in the shadows and the girls would be screaming, 'That's HIM! That's HIM!' 'Who?' 'HIM!'" They both laughed.

"I've evolved a lot since then," Masai said.

"What do the girls call you now?" Glacia asked, her well-manicured fingers toying with her hair.

"Wrath Da Spitacular," Masai said smoothly, fastening her with a sexy but masculine half-lidded look.

Just then, Masai's crew emerged, breaking the sexual intrigue. Punchlyne and Khansepp exchanged wanton glances of approval with Masai regarding Glacia. Nikki Swagg didn't view her the same.

"We go on in about a half-hour upstairs," Nikki said to Masai as her eyes swept Glacia up and down with contempt. "Meet us at the third-floor stage in fifteen."

Nikki rolled her eyes and walked stiffly off with Punchlyne and Khansepp. Masai shrugged. Glacia just shook her head.

"Remember when all I could make were snowballs?" Glacia said as she drew his gaze down to her feet. "Watch."

Glacia floated her hand above the back of one of her stilettos. Vaporous air emitted from it and quickly formed a razor-sharp scythe made of ice on the back of her heels. Masai nodded, impressed. Glacia quickly made it dissipate away just as a gruff-edged black man, Guerrilla, approached.

"I just love them ice heels, Glacia," Guerrilla said, taking a quick snort from a vial of cocaine. "When you gonna let me make 'em reach for the ceiling?"

Masai reacted, squaring off. "Ever been punched in the mouth for sayin' something stupid?"

"Don't feed into it, Boo," Glacia said as she put a calming hand on Masai's chest. "He's not worth it."

"Yeah, don't feed, Boo," Guerrilla mocked, exposing the gun beneath his shirt. "It ain't worth it."

Nearby patrons backed away. The Get Dat Gwap Clique was suddenly there, surrounding Guerrilla threateningly. He sneered back a shit-eating grin. This was right up his alley.

Nikki exchanged a discreet look with Masai as she drew up a gun from her purse. Masai shook his head "no". Nikki relented.

"Guys, we don't want any trouble," said Earth Angel as he emerged, an unassuming white guy dressed in painted-on attire. He placed a calming hand on Guerrilla's shoulder. He swatted it off.

"I can handle this, Earth Angel," Glacia said as she caressed Guerrilla's upper arm. "Guys like Guerrilla, I just give the 'cold shoulder'." From her touch, an extreme wave of cold ran from Guerrilla's shoulder to his elbow.

"B-B-Bitch" escaped lowly from Guerrilla's mouth as he stomped away, rubbing his arm briskly. Approaching security hesitantly turned away as patrons resumed their partying. Glacia then turned to Masai and flashed him a kittenish smile.

"Nice to know you still feel the need to protect me."

Just then, Kid Hardkore traipsed up, looking as if he was being called to his execution.

"Excuse me, Glacia," Hardkore muttered, "I, uh, well the thing is… Would you like to dance?"

"Of course, Corey," Glacia said, angling back to Masai. "See you in a little bit? Catch up on old times?"

Masai nodded in acknowledgement. Glacia then turned and swished away with Hardkore, who was inches shorter than her stilettoed frame. Masai's eyes, still glued on Glacia, seemed to palpably say…something. She looked back. "It's good to be seen by you."

***

99

On the dance floor, Hoodrat was twerking and grinding all over her partner like she was auditioning for a soft porn rap video. Her gyrating invited Guerrilla to dance up behind and grab hold of her bouncing booty. Sandwiched between them, Hoodrat loved it.

Guerrilla's dancing slowed as he glanced over at Glacia's ample butt swinging to the music. Impelled by a lustful urge, he boldly flittered up to it. Glacia stiffened as his pelvic region pushed up against her.

"Look, I tried to be nice," Glacia said severely. "Back off!"

Kid Hardkore flanked Guerrilla as he tried to pour on his brutish charm. "Aw baby, I was just --"

"Do it again, hear?" Glacia said daringly. Guerrilla wisely stalked away and vanished into the crowd. Glacia and Hardkore resumed dancing.

Masai treaded along the dance floor's perimeter, his heart harboring a secret thrill of anxiety as he coolly scanned for Glacia. He was feeling her, this time in an adult way. At that moment, he couldn't think of nothing but how the little chubby girlfriend of his youth became the caked-up goddess he was now sweatin'.

Masai finally targeted Glacia's hypnotically swaying hips in his scope. The intensity of his gaze drew her attention. Their eyes held on each other a magnetized moment as the song ended and segued into another, a smooth hedonistic beat. Glacia slowed then stopped dancing.

"Corey, you mind if I sit this one out?"

"Uh no," Hardkore muttered, "It's okay."

Hardkore politely marched off, unaware that she had restarted dancing. But this time, it was different. Sensual. Seductive. Summoning.

Masai traipsed over, letting his stroll manifest into a harmonious swing behind her. Glacia backed up, grinding into him. After a moment she faced him, the heat between them apparent. Glacia cradled his face tenderly as his hands explored the contour of her body...then on her butt...their eyes locked, lips, so close...

Sudden gunshots. Chilling screams.

Masai instinctively put himself between Glacia and the scattering crowd. With a sudden look of alarm, he grabbed her hand and moved through to the source of the calamity.

On the other side of the club, Masai and Glacia pushed through to see Punchlyne, Khansepp and Nikki Swagg lying slain in pooling blood. Masai's face grew hardened as he stared at his crew's lifeless bodies a moment. He then turned to Glacia. "Let's get outta here."

***

Inside of Masai's car, R&B music played softly through a delicate haze of static. Masai was behind the wheel toking on a blunt while Glacia sat beside him making playing cards dance flashily off her fingertips. A pensive yet comfortable silence existed between them as they stared deadpan at the snowflakes that blanketed the windshield in white.

"I shoulda took care of dude when I had the chance," Masai finally said, the entrancing effect of the weed seeming to make him feel good, angry and mournful all at once.

"There was nothing you could do," Glacia said. "Guerrilla is a nut job and he had a gun and powers you don't even know about. It's not your fault."

Masai blew out a cloud of smoke. "It's always my fault."

Glacia searched his face a moment as she waited for him to continue, not exactly sure what he meant.

"Life has cut you so deep, Boo," Glacia said, caressing his face ever so gently. "It didn't draw blood, but it left you in a whirlwind of pain."

Masai leaned back and closed his eyes, surrendering to her affection. He couldn't remember the last time his spirit had been at peace and this was just what he needed. But before he could settle in and enjoy it, his focus zeroed in on the news segment that had replaced the music:

"In other news, mutant guerrilla-cult leader Osiris Jackson will be executed by lethal injection tomorrow afternoon..."

"I wish you could go away with me --" Masai shushed Glacia with a finger as he sat up, focusing intently.

"Osiris Jackson was convicted of hundreds of murders spanning two decades. Now back to that station that gives you more music, less talk --" Masai turned off the radio. Glacia reacted to his distress.

"What's wrong?"

"Nothin'," Masai said dismissively. "Look, I gotta bounce. Where can I drop you off?"

Glacia was confused. "Drop me off? Why? What's up?"

"I gotta go see about somethin'," Masai said.

"We haven't seen each other since forever," Glacia said. "Now you're leaving me?"

"I forgot I got some important shit I gotta handle."

"Let me come with you," Glacia said.

Masai stubbed out the weed in the ashtray. "This is somethin' I gotta do solo."

FIFTEEN

And Thus Saith

A stylish limousine made tracks in the afternoon's snow-sloshed streets heading toward downtown Philadelphia. In the back of the limo, a now distinguished-looking Aries was talking into an elite cell phone, Lilith beside him. Still saturated with KLA swagger, it was apparent that Aries had moved up quite considerably in the world. He hung up the phone and then directed his attention across to Dr. Tucci, who was pouring himself a drink.

"The acquisitions of the natural resource companies by Empyrean Ventures have been finalized. Has your team completed the construction of the mass teleportation device?"

"The TPZ One-Thousand is ready to transport the commodities to our off-world importers," Tucci replied.

"Good," Aries said. He then regarded Lilith who was staring out of the window as Club Kindred whizzed by.

"Are you sure this is a good idea," Aries said, "Our going to see Osiris be executed?"

"Driver, pull over," Lilith said. The limousine parked close to the curb. "Osiris is the final connection Masai has to prophecy. I want to relish all hope of salvation expiring with his last breath."

Lilith looked from the car door to Aries. Getting the message, Aries exited the limousine. Lilith then glared at Tucci. He downed the rest of his drink and got out of the car. The limo peeled off, leaving Aries and Tucci standing on the cold inner-city street corner.

***

In an execution chamber, a death-appointed Osiris was strapped to an execution table. Although his eyes still glimmered with remnants of revolutionary pugnacity, his face wore the signs of someone struggling to retain their sanity.

Masai, dressed as a medical technician, stepped forward and inspected the straps. Osiris cranked his neck forward as they stared at each other with a strange intimacy. Before Osiris could say anything, Masai stepped back, and the table was erected. The curtain was then drawn back to reveal the large viewing room window. Lilith was among several dozen witnesses observing as the Warden approached Osiris.

"Osiris Jackson," the Warden bellowed, "Any last words?"

"Y'all scrambled my mind, suppressed my powers," Osiris said. "I told 'em straight up. Don't let that boy go to no public school. He'll grow up an eagle who thinks he's a chicken. I said it. Now it's dead. Y'all devils are next."

Osiris turned away humming a tune as the witnesses grinned at his presumed schizophrenic remarks. The Warden then signaled a guard to power up the lethal injection machine.

The guard reached for a lever and a hand grabbed his wrist. He resisted and half-turned -- Masai drove a punch to the guard's face. He then broke him down with a stunning combination, picked him up overhead and heaved him at the viewing window. Witnesses scattered and hit the floor as the guard crashed through amid a rain of glass.

The Warden swiftly drew his firearm. Masai parried, elbow-smashing him in the face. Masai grappled the Warden's wrist and flipped him through the air, grabbing the gun at once. Masai spun, firing. Three guards fell, dead. He then disassembled the gun and rushed over to Osiris. "Dad!"

"I knew one day you'd come for me," Osiris said with tears blurring his smiling eyes. Masai proceeded to remove the execution paraphernalia, hoisted up his father and crossed to the exit door.

A dozen or so footsteps echoed outside the room, getting closer. Masai placed Osiris down, picked up a shard of glass then gripped the Warden up hostage-style, glass to his throat.

"Take it easy, son," the Warden said with a forced calm. Masai spun the Warden around as a shield just as a wave of CMTF agents stormed in, aiming and advancing.

"Down on the floor, asshole!" The lead agent barked as agents angled in, forcing Masai to drag the Warden back against the wall. "Don't tempt me, motherfucker! Get the fuck down! Now!"

Masai peered through his wild locs from behind the Warden at the army against him. He was trapped like a rat. Masai scanned around frantically, searching, watching as the last of the stragglers were being hustled out. Terror crept over him as his eyes held fast to someone in the crowd…

In Masai's field of vision, Lilith's pale skin was grotesquely satanic. Her widened eyes were rimmed with jaundice and in her mouth was flesh-ripping fangs.

Masai tried to swallow what it all meant as his former social worker was hustled out. He roved the glass visors of the agents, their faces demoniacal in his sight. Masai then slanted to his father, who was fixed on the floor smiling cryptically.

"Kill these devils, son," Osiris said, his voice a dead icy hiss. "Kill them all."

"I'm not going to tell you again," the lead agent growled, "Let the Warden go and get the fuck down! Now!"

Masai was no longer paying attention to the lead agent's mandate. He was lost in the depths of his own mind. "Muthafuckas…"

Suddenly, the steel exit door behind the agents ominously slammed shut and an unnatural wind picked up in the death chamber. Everyone exchanged chilling glances.

Masai's celestial eye flared and nightmarishly swept the room. Fragmented glass missiles darted into agent's wrists and hands, impelling them to release their weapons. Masai slung the Warden hard to the floor, the cosmic winds blowing his clothes and locs.

"Devils wanna kill me, my family..."

"You don't have to do this, son," the Warden appealed, his face fiendish in Masai's scope. "What is it that you want?"

Masai had a moment of calm as if his consciousness was kicking into a hyper-combat readiness. Then --

"I want all of y'all," Masai said grimly, **"TO DIE."**

A haunting moment as the words stirred through the air. Suddenly, the Warden began to clutch his neck as if something noxious was cutting off his airway. Confusion escalated into panic as his face reddened, greened and blued. His bulging eyes beseeched the room. Agents were going through similar distress, flailing wildly and crucially gasping for air. Masai glared with savage vigilance as one by one they all collapsed to the floor, dead.

Masai dashed over to his father who was lying motionless amid the carnage, his limbs askew and limp. A hot wave of panic rolled through Masai's body as he collapsed to the floor, his grief-stricken face saying it all.

"No, no, no, Dad...I didn't mean you...Dad, no..." Masai cried as he cradled Osiris' head, a webbing of saliva between his lips. More agents busted in. Masai didn't resist...

***

Stanley was shoveling snow out front of Mrs. Ortiz's store. Suddenly, the wind picked up as obsidian clouds roiled overhead. Mrs. Ortiz came out and looked up into the sky. They then exchanged a knowing look and smile. "It is time."

Stanley's shovel fell to the ground as the organic matter of their bodies became less compact, converting into vaporous energy particles. Clothes dropped to the snow as their astral forms ascended into the sky…

The orange sun gleamed on the tail of a French Airliner as it flew toward an airport. The jet teetered suddenly, throwing everyone off balance. A flight attendant trekked into the cockpit, watching with horror as the pilot and co-pilot's bodies decomposed right before her, their vague essences ascending through the roof. The flight attendant screamed as the jet began to plummet rapidly. The plane collided with the tarmac and exploded. Dozens of astral forms escalated from the wreckage and into the air…

In Nigeria, four children frolicked in the African breeze. A little girl tagged a boy and ran behind a tree on the right side. In an instant, her astral form mounted out from the left, rising into the heavens. The essence of the boy running at once became airy and elevated with the other two children…

In the sky, an infinite number of astral forms from all over the earth converged, assembling into a diaphanous cloud. It was easily three miles across, growing larger as more translucent forms joined. It focused into a prodigious swirling vortex that increased with violent fervor. When the last entity conjoined, it exploded with a deafening thunderclap. Then…

Absolute silence. Through the decreasing haze the earth returned to its normal state.

***

Back in Philadelphia, there was pandemonium. Thousands crowded the thoroughfares madly trampling anything in their path. Grid-locked traffic contrasted the spirited horn honking as gunfire rippled through the night air, inciting lunacy on the riotous streets.

In a hotel suite overlooking the madness below, Dr. Tucci cradled a drink in one hand and a cigarette in the other.

"To the end," Tucci said as he toasted the sky and knocked it back. A knock at the door. Tucci walked over and opened it. Henry Murray, the shape-shifted identity that Supreme Maffmattixx had assumed years earlier was standing there.

"Hello, Tucci."

"Henry," Tucci said, his sloshed face squinting recognition. "Man, you look great. Haven't seen you in almost two decades."

As Henry was led into the room, he began to shapeshift into Supreme Maffmattixx, sporting a black leather jacket adorned with numerical-shaped jewels.

"It was just yesterday to me."

Tucci's cigarette, drink and jaw dropped to the floor. He made a beeline to the door. Tucci suddenly backed in with Johann Faust and several Hands of Wrath members pressing behind him.

"Sixteen years ago," Maffmattixx said, closing in on Tucci. "The clone you were working on. I wanna know who it was."

"I don't know what you're talking about," Tucci said.

Maffmattixx shapeshifted into Ming and materialized a blade. She pressed it against Tucci's throat.

"Whatever you do to me will be ticklish by comparison," Tucci winced out. Ming pushed another knife firmly into his groin. "Then you'll die laughing."

Tucci bitched up. "Okay! Okay!"

Ming eased off and reformed back into Maffmattixx. Tucci checked his crotch for damage then picked up sheets of paper from under a bottle of Hennessey. Faust snatched the papers from him.

"What the hell is this?" Faust said, leafing through the papers. "Suzuki Trading, McCray Smelting, Motumbo Incorporated... These are all refineries of precious metals."

"Trail the path of the commodities," Tucci said. "That's where you will find the one who will make your most surreal, paranoid dream horrifically real."

Faust moved in close to Maffmattixx. "He's full of shit."

"Maybe," Maffmattixx said as Tucci breathed in his frustration and exhaled his fear.

"Listen, you guys gotta protect me. That's one of the things you Hands of Wrath guys do, right?"

"Protect you from who?" Maffmattixx said.

"From who?" Tucci said incredulously. **"VAMPYRO!"**

SIXTEEN

VAMPYRO

A warm ray of sun suffused from the skylight above as Archbishop Francis prepared drinks at the bar inside of Von Pyros' grand and regal office. The stone walls were bare except for a bas relief of Dorian Von Pyros and a bevy of enchantresses that dwelled above the stylish sofa.

Dr. Tucci suddenly stepped in through an opaque-glass partition with a sense of urgency. "Where's Von Pyros?"

"In worship," Archbishop Francis said.

Tucci plopped down on the sofa. "you're telling me our security's been risked and he's in no rush to see me?

"Relax, Tucci," Francis said, handing him a drink.

"Tell him he can pray later," Tucci said, wolfing it down. "We'd be well advised to deal with this situation now."

Just then, Von Pyros entered, followed by a dozen members of the secret order of the Brotherhood of the

Vampyrians, former President Reynolds among them. He strolled over and sat close to Tucci on the sofa.

"Why are you so anxious all of a sudden?" Reynolds said. "You didn't have a problem when Embryxx Industries was receiving hundreds of millions. You thinking of pulling out?"

Tucci looked around at the consortium with a strickened look, stopping at Von Pyros.

"I-It's just Johann Faust, a-and the KLA shapeshifter I told you about from last night. It raises some serious questions about the projects' security, my anonymity, know what I mean?"

"The first supernatural blow has been struck and your cowardice is impeding my progress," Von Pyros said. "Operation Triple-Six is operating behind schedule and my fury will be exacted on those I deem responsible."

Tucci swallowed hard the two lumps in his throat as he sat there with an empty sack. "The product has reached its maturity, ready for Phase One."

"Good," Von Pyros said. He then flagged Tucci over and steered him toward the glass partition.

"Don't be concerned with Faust. And Supreme Maffmattixx's shapeshifting and time-jumping abilities have made him quite difficult to locate over the years. You leading him to Empyrean City was quite advantageous for us. We'll be able to keep a watchful eye on him here."

Tucci about-faced on the other side of the partition.

"I knew I could count on you, Gerald," Von Pyros said. "You have always been a valued friend in the struggle. I won't forget that." Von Pyros closed the partition in his face.

"Think he's going to hold up?" Reynolds asked.

Von Pyros offered nothing as Archbishop Francis approached with a tray filled with glasses of champagne, handing him one. The Brotherhood of the Vampyrian czars then began reaching for the rest of the glasses.

"The catching up in the clouds of the Kindred souls has earmarked the dawning of a new age," Von Pyros said, raising his glass high. "With the maturation of my genetic replicate confirmed, vindication is finally upon us."

The bigwigs clanged their glasses together and sipped.

"The disappearances have generated the kind of worldwide anxiety we'd anticipated," Archbishop Francis said. "Religious institution attendance is at an all-time high."

"Cities in need of restoration, food, exploitation of natural resources," well-groomed bankster Jasper Knight said, "The people of the world will have to foot the bill as our profits soar through the roof."

"We seem to have a little problem in Washington," Reynolds said. "A couple of trading commissioners reluctant to adjust their regulations."

"Dr. Medeevyl," Von Pyros said to the androgynous bio-weapons specialist toying with a frisky white mouse, "Think you can travel to the Capital and give them second thoughts with a painful viral infection for their families?"

"It will be my pleasure," Dr. Medeevyl sneered.

"Also, I'm afraid we're going to have to give an explanation for the disappearances," Archbishop Francis said. "We can't let the masses discern its esoteric significance."

"We could demonize the Kindreds that refuse to sign our peace agreement," Knight said. "After all, they're already considered mutant-terrorists."

Von Pyros pivoted to smooth media mogul Jacob Sterling. "I assume you've centralized control of the media, Sterling. You look quite at ease."

"The propaganda machine is in full effect," Sterling said.

Von Pyros convened in his monogrammed chair, his expression one of sublime content. "I've waited an eternity for this moment in time, setting the stage for the ultimate battle."

"What about the Prophesied One?" Knight asked.

"What about him?" Von Pyros said. "He is incapacitated by his own tortured mind, where the true battle takes place."

Just then, Lilith entered and whispered in Von Pyros' ear. Angered, he pounded the desk with his fist.

***

Inside of a lavish penthouse in Empyrean City, a party was taking place. Loud music. Coke-covered tables. Beautiful model-types galore. Von Pyros entered with Lilith, stopping just inside the room. His gaze wandered across and riveted on Dr. Spinn in a Jacuzzi. Dr. Spinn had a top dollar bottle of Dom in one hand and a blonde bombshell in the other. He was lascivious with both.

"Do you know why I am such a happy creature?" Von Pyros asked as he approached the hot tub.

"Yes, I believe so," Dr. Spinn slurred, "You've got Kindred representatives and world leaders to agree to sign the peace treaty as you establish a New World Order."

"Precisely," Von Pyros said. "And as long as I am charged with writing the charter, I've got the whole world in my hands." Von Pyros then began to sing with child-like elocution. "I've-got-the-whole-wide-world-in-my-hands."

Dr. Spinn grinned sloppily. Everyone else laughed tensely.

"You know the only thing that worries me?" Von Pyros queried, his tone shifting.

"I'm not really sure," Dr. Spinn said.

"Take a wild guess... Masai remaining self-contained perhaps?" Dr. Spinn began to stammer nervously. "But with each passing moment, his fucking power is increasing!!"

Everyone sprang from the Jacuzzi, leaving Dr. Spinn solo. Von Pyros looked nightmarishly upward. A nefarious chain suddenly materialized from the ceiling and coiled around Dr. Spinn's neck. It lifted his thong-clad frame into the air, his legs dripping and pinwheeling wildly.

Von Pyros crossed to him; his voice soft but forbidding. "He was supposed to be neutralized."

Dr. Spinn spoke in a blubbering choked gurgle. "Master, please...have mercy..."

"Your behavioral modification methods are useless," Von Pyros said grimly as he opened his shirt, revealing a subsisting eye in the center of his chest. "And so are you."

Von Pyros' chest-eye crackled and fired an occult blast that engulfed Dr. Spinn with a damnable energy. It looked like fire but appeared to be deathly cold. Dr. Spinn screamed as the blast freezer-burned away his clothes, glasses and features. The chain dropped Dr. Spinn, leaving his charred remains on the floor. Everyone was horrified.

"Oh well," Von Pyros shrugged, "What is combat without adversaries?"

"There is another way," Lilith said, plucking the "Arcane Mirrors" card. "When an axe enters the forest, the trees see the axe handle as one of them. Masai must become one of us."

***

In a stifling prison cell, a shirtless Masai snapped up from his bunk, his face and muscles bathed in sweat. Except for the metal sink and commode, he was alone.

Masai swung to the side of his bunk, slowly focusing on reality. He ran his fingers through his locs, trying to shake the remorseful ache from his stomach and mind, but couldn't. Over the years, he tried to retain a small level of optimism about his oracular fate, and to a degree had been successful in a hazy kind of way. But there was no ignoring the fact that his father was murdered from the sheer power of his words. "It should have been me," he thought, since he felt dead already.

With a growl of frustration, Masai struck his fist against the nearest concrete wall, bashing through it like tissue paper. He pulled back his hand and looked at it with hesitance and wide-eyed surprise. A reddish-orange tiger paw was on the end of his wrist with forepaw pads on the underside and flesh-ripping claws on each digit.

Masai critiqued the paw thoroughly, focusing on the slight ghost-like after-image that tailed after each motion. His father manifesting telekinetic blades on his hands suddenly visualized in his head:

"Greater, a thousand times greater things you'll be able to do."

With realization sinking in, Masai willed the tiger claw away and his hand reverted to normal. He then made a fist and flexed his mind. Suddenly, the flexor knuckles of his fingers began to extend and protrude into venom-perforating fangs. Cat-like eyes appeared on either side of the fist and olive-green scales carpeted the entire hand, completing the formation of a telekinetic snake's head.

Masai stood and marveled at the snake head a moment as it writhed and spat rabidly. He then began to construct kung-fu formations with it and before he even realized it, he was executing snake-style techniques against imaginary attackers.

By degrees, he began to employ the other animals of the Shaolin kung fu system; the tiger's ferocious claw, the lethal beak of a pecking crane, the mighty fist of a monkey and the carnivorous jaws of a flame-spitting dragon.

Each fantastic strike became more powerful as he cranked up the speed and intensity, going punishingly hard against inner opponents that he couldn't see, immersed in a subconscious battle that he was losing. After a while, Masai collapsed on the bunk with his reasoning clouded by anger, guilt and self-pity.

Then, in what he considered a stroke of insight, Masai decided to push his past deeper into the caverns of his mind and concluded that he could not hurt anyone else if he stayed locked away and never vocalized another word again.

"Let's go," a voice boomed outside of the cell door. Masai popped up and gave a snake-eyed glare to the face that was at the door's window. "You got a meeting."

SEVENTEEN

EMPYREAN FORCE

An armada of freight trucks exited a highway and turned up a sweeping road that led to the front gate of Mount Stronghold. As the convoy disappeared past the gate, Supreme Maffmattixx materialized out of thin air and keenly looked skyward. "Six thirty-nine." He then strolled to the front gate where a guard was moving into position to block his entrance.

"I'm Supreme Maffmattixx. I was told to meet with —"

"Commander Kinetis," a voice bellowed. Maffmattixx looked over and saw Cassius Monteszuma, now referred to as KINETIS, approaching. Bio-metal alloy and cybernetics now overlayed the left side of his body and face, masking his horrific burns. Kinetis' thermoscopic eye gave Maffmattixx the once over, his jacket's twinkling jewels eye-catching. Kinetis' look disclosed that he didn't care for him very much.

"You may have been referred by one of the corporate bigwigs," Kinetis said, brushing past Maffmattixx's extended hand, "But you've amassed exactly zero hours in Empyrean Force. You're a newborn, a blank slate, waiting for me to feed you, lead you and bleed you." Kinetis then lead Maffmattixx to the glass elevator.

Inside of the elevator, Kinetis spoke to Maffmattixx over his shoulder as they submerged into Empyrean City.

"Originally the Counter Mutant-Terrorism Force, Empyrean Force has been re-designated to also deal with issues related to the presence of alien beings. We're like a cross between Delta Force and the X-Files, only with superpowers. We detect, analyze and take direct action against mutant and possible extra-terrestrial threats in a confidential manner."

Kinetis' words fell on deaf ears as Maffmattixx's eyes followed the fleet of trucks down the main thoroughfare.

"You like being emancipated?" Kinetis asked.

"What?" Maffmattixx barked then caught himself. "Sir?"

Kinetis smirked, surmising that only a mutant-terrorist would have taken offense to that.

"Free," Kinetis said. "Preserving the freedom we cherish requires a galvanized military force. And if there is a mu-terrorist revolt or an alien distress here or off-world, we must be prepared."

Kinetis and Maffmattixx moved through a lively sector of the revamped plaza. They slowed to a stop at the last passageway christened with the "Omega" symbol.

"This is us," Kinetis said. "Omega Squadron."

"Twenty-one insurgences prevented last year worldwide," Maffmattixx chimed. "Up thirty-eight point-two percent from the previous year."

"That's right," Kinetis said, slightly taken aback by his preciseness. "And we've prevented over a hundred by good database analysis with no unnecessary mutant hocus-pocus. You feelin' me, dawg?"

Maffmattixx shot him a look from the condescending remark just as Hoodrat flounced over, displaying her chasm-deep cleavage and that oh-so familiar ass-crack.

"'Sup, I'm Hoodrat," she said coyly.

"No kiddin'," Kinetis said. "Any fool can see that."

Hoodrat sucked her teeth just as Natasha rushed over. She took Kinetis aside and whispered in his ear. The news rocked Kinetis. "Who else knows about this?"

"No one here in Empyrean City," Natasha said. "Just the rest of the world, what's left of it."

Off to the side, Hoodrat sucked her thumb as she eyeballed the glittering integers on Maffmattixx's jacket. "So, what are your powers? Calculus? Quantum Physics?'"

"Something like that," Maffmattixx said dismissively, focusing on a handful of haloed prisoners parading in single file, two android sentries monitoring them. "Who are they?"

"Mutant prisoners sent to be evaluated for attitude adjustment," Hoodrat said. "If they know what I know, they'll play the game or end up gumming baby food from here on out." Hoodrat pressed her breasts against him as she whispered in close. "You don't have to worry about me, though. Their rehab methods never stopped me from being a friendly girl."

Maffmattixx stepped back from her just as Kinetis slid back over, directing his attention to Hoodrat.

"He's with the survey team. Brief him for intergalactic simulation in one hour... And get a proper goddamn uniform!" Kinetis then turned and slipped into an elevator with Natasha.

"He wasn't worried about no proper uniform when I was..." Hoodrat caught herself and moved on. "So what's your call sign?"

"Supreme Maffmattixx." Hoodrat locked arms with him. "Pretty long. What can I call you for short?" He snatched his arm back. "Supreme Maffmattixx."

***

Kinetis and Natasha moved at a brisk pace down the hall.

"What caused the disappearances?" Kinetis asked.

"Not sure," Natasha said, stopping at a pressurized door. "We never detected a signal. But there is one possibility."

Natasha eye-dentiscanned and the door flew open. The duo entered and crossed to a table where Cyber and Freeloader were looking over a three-dimensional hologram of a complex superstructure with a massive screen.

"What's this?" Kinetis asked.

"A mass teleportation device," Cyber said. "Compliments of Hands of Wrath leader Johann Faust."

"Teleportation machines don't grow from trees," Kinetis said. "Where'd they get the technology?"

"Dr. Tucci and his team developed it for space travel," Freeloader said. "But his people claim they've only been able to transmit information, not organic matter."

"If they're working with the world's most dangerous adversary, what else would you expect them to say?" Kinetis said. "That bastard Faust makes Hitler look like an infant Gandhi." Kinetis touched his cybernetic ear and spoke. "Get me Von Pyros."

EIGHTEEN

ARIES THE CANCER

"Yes, it's fine," Von Pyros said to the receptionist's face on his desk's monitor. "Send Kinetis up."

"Right away, sir," the receptionist said, her image disappearing from the screen. Von Pyros then regarded Aries who was seated across from his desk.

"So, Aries," Von Pyros said, pulling out two cigars, handing him one. "I understand that I have you to thank for supervising the consummation of my clone, as well as securing the lion's share of our business throughout the solar system. Good work."

"Thank you, sir," Aries said. "Our advances in trading technology have allowed me to also obtain deals in Andromeda Galaxy and there's potential beyond."

"Grabbing the bull by the horns," Von Pyros said as he came from behind his desk and lit Aries' cigar. "I like that. But you must not get too cocky. Andromedans thrive on excitement and are very crafty in business, so go slowly." Von Pyros then directed his attention across the room to Lilith, who was plucking a tarot card from the patterned spread arrangement on a table.

"Ambition, treachery, greed," Von Pyros said, "Qualities that have made Aries one of the Brotherhood's best friends, wouldn't you say, Lilith?"

Lilith held the "Jack of Two Faces" card between her gloved fingers. "It seems that our relationship with one of our other best friends has run its course. Tucci has sought refuge with Faust and the Hands of Wrath."

Von Pyros' face turned grim just as there was a knock on the door. An assistant allowed Kinetis in and exited. "Sorry to bother you, sir," Kinetis said, "But we have a situation."

"Kinetis, my trusted ally. What can I do for you?"

"Johann Faust," Kinetis said. "He's creating devastation of biblical proportions topside."

"Yes, such a tragedy," Von Pyros said with an artificial compassion. "When I know something, you'll know. Just have your team prepared and battle ready. Anything else?"

Kinetis gave a cursory glance around and saw Aries staring at him smugly. Without a glimmer of recognition, he glared back, sizing Aries up through his own prejudiced lens; on the surface, aristocratic and elegant, but underneath a maverick who reminded him of an issue he wanted to address.

"The new agent, Supreme Maffmattixx," Kinetis said. "There's no file on him anywhere. He stayed completely off the grid. I think he's a mutant-terrorist. I suggest he be prepped for rehab and counter-radicalization."

The assistant suddenly appeared at the partition and stuck her head in. "Sir, your guest is waiting."

"I'll be right there," Von Pyros said. The assistant backed out. "I have every confidence in Maffmattixx's abilities, so judge his competence, not his swagger or the jewels on his jacket. Now, if there isn't anything else, I have much business to attend to, so…"

"No sir," Kinetis said reflexively. He wanted to say more, but instead exited, confounded by Von Pyros' blasé demeanor about such a grave situation.

"Questions, so many questions," Von Pyros said as he re-convened behind his desk. "I believe that our Empyrean Force Commander might come down with a severe case of bereavement sooner than expected."

"Aries, your presence seemed to raise an eyebrow with him," Lilith said.

"Never met him," Aries said slyly.

"What about Supreme Maffmattixx?" Lilith asked.

"Death is the price he will pay for trying to create balance out of chaos," Von Pyros said.

"And Tucci?"

"An expendable asset," Von Pyros said, blowing out a ring of smoke. "His fate will mark the birth of Phase One."

NINETEEN

WHEN POLAR OPPOSITES SHALL MEET

A shackled Masai was force-marched through a waiting area by Skizzo then roughly shoved into a seat. Skizzo then moved to his place off to the side. Masai panned from Skizzo over to a huge hologram that floated high in the room, its images whizzing by as it channel-surfed like a television. Masai's hard look instantly altered to shock as he watched station after station flick past:

Tanks roaming American streets -- a Japanese city ravaged by flood -- protests in major cities around the world -- pundits engaged in shouting tirades --

The scene finally rested on live coverage of reporter Jordyn Martinez in front of the havoc in downtown Philadelphia:

"In Philadelphia and across the globe, millions of people have mysteriously disappeared off the face of the earth. Mania ensued as confused and frightened people took to the streets, leaving every major city on earth a war zone. These disappearances have yet to be

explained, but several citizens have offered their version of this unnatural calamity."

The scene then changed to Raheem Johnson: *"It was this bright ball up in the sky that blew up! My dog's gone, too! Damn mu-terrorists!"*

Then to Yvonne Gomez: *"If you Hands of Wrath people have my babies, return them to me! Please!"*

Then to Rocko Giambone: *"This is something out of the Bible. It sez all the saints will be marching up to Jacob's ladder! Yo, this is some scary (BLEEP!), knowwhatImsayin'?"*

Then to Tanya Scolski: *"UFOs are real. This proves it beyond a shadow of a doubt. Now all the countries of the world must forget our petty differences and become united."*

Back to Jordyn, her eyes streaming: *"From mu-terrorists to religious implications to UFO's, one thing's for sure... I never told my mother how much I love her. Reporting live from Center City, this is Jordyn Martinez for WPHZ News. Back to you, Gary."*

To Gary Dodsworth in the studio: *"Our prayers are with you, Jordyn. In a related topic, the President has issued a statement –"* The hologram suddenly burst into a pixelated mist and was gone.

Masai sat there white-knuckled, the pandemic omen seemingly confirming his secrets fears.

"Mutant-terrorists are such monsters..." a voice echoed from within the room. Masai turned and saw an utterly composed Von Pyros standing by a side entrance sealed off by velvet drapes. "Makes you wonder what's inside of people."

Von Pyros went back through the plush enclosure. Masai hesitated then followed him.

Masai stepped through and stood idly a moment, taking in the surroundings. It was a formal parlor. On the wall was a collection of books. Some of them appeared to be ancient and rare, the bindings inscribed with peculiar symbols. Masai began to move through, studying the books with interest. Von Pyros casually walked over to a chess set, the pieces amid militant combat.

"Move one of the pieces with your mind." Von Pyros said. Masai didn't respond. "Both of your parents had telekinesis, right? It should be easy for you. Try it."

Masai listlessly strolled over and looked at the chess board. A knight levitated and checked the king. Mate.

"Just as I suspected," Von Pyros said. "Your powers were passed on to you genetically. You can move and control things with your mind."

Masai shifted Von Pyros' gaze to his shackled wrists. The shackles unlocked and released, falling to the floor. Masai curled a faint sneer.

"I see Osiris' talent in you, but I also see his recklessness," Von Pyros said. "I counseled your father for years during his confinement. He also took objection to his standing as a mutant."

Masai furiously smacked books off the shelf, then lifted his shirt and pointed to the birthmark on his chest.

"I'm not no mutant, dawg!" Wrath barked telepathically at Von Pyros, gesturing with streetwise flair. *"I'm the Kindred*

immortal, Wrath the Conqueror! Like a phoenix reborn from the ashes, I was reincarnated to wrest vengeance on the fiends of darkness, you feel me?"

"You're getting defensive," Von Pyros said. "What makes more sense – you are a demigod returning to protect humanity during the end of the world, or that you are a mutant who killed his father by expelling a freak burst of psychokinetic energy due to acute stress, possibly the same stress that is preventing you from expressing yourself verbally now?"

Masai plopped in a seat, demoralized.

"You are not unique," Von Pyros said, shifting to an oddly soothing tone. "There are others, who accept their gifts and use them for the benefit of Mankind. I can help you, but only if you are willing to help yourself."

TWENTY

REAL REAL

"This is the training room," Hoodrat said as she escorted Maffmattixx into a stark room the size of a football field, a spherical control booth overhead. "Holograms are broadcast in here for simulations. Add sounds, atmospheric conditions, even smells, stuff becomes real. I mean *real* real."

As they moved through toward the rest of the Omega squad members, Maffmattixx coolly scrutinized the laser projectors and sentry guns concealed to the untrained eye.

Approaching, Axiss regarded Maffmattixx with dollar signs for eyeballs. "Mmm... Who's dude with Hoodrat?"

"Who gives a fuck," a wired Guerrilla said, outfitted with an exoskeleton and an arsenal of hi-tech weapons. Axiss dismissed him and sashayed in close to Maffmattixx.

"What's up with all the jewels?" Axiss asked.

"Each gem is associated with a specific planet according to its wavelength, augmenting my power," Maffmattixx said. "Take the planet Venus for instance –"

"Too much info," Axiss said, "How much they cost?"

Maffmattixx jeered. He then turned his attention over to Johnny Fatal, who was flashily twirling two Glocks as he leered upon Hoodrat, who was posed in a pigeon-toed-stank-booty stance taking a selfie.

"That's the devil's greatest tool, homeboy," Maffmattixx whispered to Fatal, regarding Hoodrat.

"Whatever, bro," Fatal said as he adhered the guns to his lower back. They de-materialized into tattoos just above his waistline.

A magical aperture suddenly opened above in hollow space. Everyone looked up as sorcerer Mister Mystiqal exited. He looked like a Greek God with blonde hair and blue-blood attitude to match.

"Isn't he amazing?" Earth Angel said like a pre-teen gazing upon their favorite matinee idol. Maffmattixx shot Earth Angel a look just as Mister Mystiqal touched down.

"Alas, Earth Angel," Mister Mystiqal said as he approached, hovering a foot above the floor with his arms folded imperially. "Vacationing on the mystic plane is not what it used to be."

"I'm so glad you're back... Mister Mystiqal, this is --"

"Supreme Maffmattixx," Mister Mystiqal interjected. "Revolutionary journeyman. Bound by birthright."

"What's the dilly, Mystiqal?" Maffmattixx said.

Earth Angel was perplexed. "You two know each other?"

"Ladies and gentlemen," a computerized voice boomed from above, *"This is a continuation from last week's arrival sequence. Your objective is to characterize the structure and composition of Mars and search for evidence of life. You have approximately three hours. Good luck."*

The lights abruptly shut off and there was total darkness. Illumination came back on instantly and the Omega Squad no longer appeared to be in the training room. They were now on the dark side of Mars surrounded by endless space. Two moons floated behind jagged mountain peaks off in the distance. Hyper-real.

In an instant, strong wind gusts of reddish-brown dust began to shroud the environment. Weightlessness granted everyone a graceless buoyancy as the air thinned, squelching their breaths. Everyone shivered from the rapidly decreasing temperature except Glacia, who was unaffected by the ultra-cold. Simultaneously, key members of the Omega Squad went into action:

Mister Mystiqal waved his hand. He preened as the air instantly became breathable and gravity lowered everyone to the terrain --

Axiss' body transformed a non-reflective black as she absorbed the energy from the solar winds, her body bubbling with corona orbs of various sizes --

A sudden burst of feathered wings exploded out of Earth Angel's back. He soared into the air and gestured, lessening the choking dust storm to the blow of a lover's kiss --

Glacia extended her hands and drew vapory mist into her fingertips. Frost and ice began to melt and dissipate away. The counterfeit Mars' environment was now that of earth.

"Survey team, move in," Kinetis commanded.

Johnny Fatal walked through, kicking up a cloud of dust. "Ain't nothin' ever live here, yo."

Earth Angel touched down, his wings folding neatly behind him. "You're walking in a dried-up riverbed, Johnny. Could mean water flowed here once. It's possible there is or was life."

Using her ability to see several electromagnetic bands of light, Emosha analyzed the texture and mineralogy of a huge boulder. "Judging from the quality of salinity in this boulder, the water wouldn't have been able to support humanoid life."

"Maybe there's life in the form of microorganisms under the surface," Kataklysmo said.

Maffmattixx fingered the dry land. "The core is six hundred thirty-two thousand kilometers down. Water deposits near the core might be habitable for indigenous microbes."

"Hope we don't have to go that far down," Axiss said.

"Alright, time to dig into this planet's guts," Kinetis said. "Kid Hardkore, move that rock. Axiss, Hoodrat. Excavation."

Kid Hardkore tossed the boulder aside effortlessly as Axiss generated two solar-radiated axes out of thin air. She then led off, shredding through the terrain like hot butter.

Hoodrat growled at once and her face began transforming like the rodent of her name. Fangs and hair emerged, and her fingernails tapered into iron-ripping claws. She then "scratched" the air, her five fingers creating furrowed rifts in hollow space. Five rat-like entities, the Hoodrats, charged out of the rifts crazily. Although they resembled their forerunner, three of her broods were suggested hybrids of Kataklysmo, Guerrilla and Kinetis.

"Come on, bitches," Hoodrat said to her spawns as she took off. The Hoodrats ran over with their predecessor and began clearing out the hole with unrivaled devotion.

Emosha swapped glances between Kinetis and what appeared to be his hulking rat-bastard child. With a jealous glare, she gestured over her shoulder -- SCHINGGG! Emosha unsheathed a photon sword from an invisible pocket dimension. She looked fiercely at Kinetis. He angled to her, puzzled. Emosha rolled her eyes and kept it moving.

***

Von Pyros and Masai traipsed across a glass crosswalk in the sector, with Masai hitching his sagging pants up frequently. Von Pyros studied Masai's 'hood habit curiously, regarding it as an absurd inconvenience.

"Style and fashion does not have to be a badge of delinquency."

Masai jeered. He hitched up his pants and kept walking as several CIA-looking suits approached Von Pyros, stalling him. Von Pyros greeted them as they spoke in hushed tones.

Masai, now far ahead, looked around, his gaze drawn to a huge steel door with a thin shaft of crimson light streaming out from under it. He headed toward it curiously…

***

Inside the training room, the Omega squad were scattered about performing their simulation protocol. Mister Mystiqal hovered over to Maffmattixx, who was collecting soil samples.

"Do you believe you will find the one that you seek here, in this particular time and space?" Mystiqal asked.

Maffmattixx straightened up. "Why don't you keep it one-hunnit and tell me, B."

"Fate must design the time that is to come for herself."

Wrong answer. Maffmattixx went back to work. Mystiqal looked upward to a comet streaking across the cosmos, his mystic vision allowing him to peer through to the control booth above. Inside the control booth, technicians were operating the main console, their faces kindling electric red from the dozens of viewport screens that displayed all angles of the counterfeit Mars. Mystiqal focused on Von Pyros and the suits as they entered, quietly playing the background.

"The globe holders have worked tirelessly in their efforts to quell the mark bearer's power," Mystiqal said. "If you find him, do you believe you can help free his mind?"

In close proximity, a doorway suddenly opened in the middle of hollow space. Mystiqal and Maffmattixx watched as the sillhouetted figure of Masai stepped through. Maffmattixx squinted back at Mystiqal. "Word up."

Masai slowly turned in a circle, intoxicated by wavering sensations. One moment he looked as if he was about to cry, then he would burst out laughing. It was as if every atom in his body was a part of this universe, as if he was home.

"So I hear you're the seed of Osiris and Ashanti Jackson," Maffmatixx's voice echoed from behind Masai. He about-faced out of his stupor and saw Maffmattixx standing there.

"Don't sweat it. Consider me a finder of lost divinity." Maffmattixx then began to circle, sizing him up.

"Kindred revolutionaries battling demons. Pretty deep stuff. Didn't rub off? The duty? The legacy?"

Masai didn't bother acknowledging him, his attention focused elsewhere off in the distance...

At the excavation area, Guerrilla was prankishly smacking the face down-ass up rumps of the Hoodrats like the Three Stooges. As he trotted away from the blushing vermins, he spotted Masai glaring at him with pent-up hatred.

"Sonofabitch," Guerrilla muttered as he drew his sophisticated hand cannon, lightning fast. He fired at Masai, a volley of perfect kill shots -- Masai simultaneously raised his hand. The bullets froze in the air inches from him then fell to the ground. Masai then looked sharply upward. Laser projectors sizzled and exploded. Sentry guns locked and loaded, zeroing in on Guerrilla. Mars dissipated into the barren training room as the guns opened fire. Masai telekinetically made a relentless barrage of rounds chase a fleeing Guerrilla. Everyone else tried desperately to get out of the way.

Guerrilla lunged and amazingly phased inside of Johnny Fatal's body. Fatal/Guerrilla swiftly drew his tatted glocks and began firing back blindly at Masai on the move --

-- Masai gestured, making the bullets take a deft U-turn and return toward the guns from whence they came --

Guerrilla sprang out of Fatal, who instinctively tattooed himself to the floor as bullets pinged across him --

Guerrilla then plunged headfirst inside of Kid Hardkore. Slugs bounced off Hardkore's tough frame as he barbarically paced toward Masai...

Sentry guns abruptly shut down as a current of energy washed over Masai's body. The energy fused internally into his tendons and tissue, augmenting his mass, strength and speed. Masai flexed his muscles, admiring his might just as Hardkore plodded up --

An epic exchange of blows jumped off, vicious and brutal. Masai's hands were a blur as he landed savage combinations while Hardkore pounded Masai's psychokinetic-imbued structure like jackhammers.

Eluding a punch, Masai increased his hand to a catcher's mitt-sized monkey fist, a ghostly after effect trailing his mighty swing -- KAPOW! Masai landed a murderous haymaker that caved Hardkore's chest in and sent him flying. He sailed about fifty feet and smashed hard into a thick metal wall, denting it with his muscular impression. A shaken Guerrilla crawled out of Hardkore and collapsed.

Teeming with adrenaline and cold fury, Masai was ready to purge what he felt was confusing and ugly within himself on others just as a familiar sweet voice echoed behind him.

"Be easy, Boo…easy…" Masai nightmarishly pivoted, and his eyes fell on Glacia. Her placid aura and beauty had an instantaneous effect on him. His intensity subsided and his body returned to normal size.

"Ohmigod!" Glacia exclaimed as she hugged him tightly just before blitzing him with a gazillion questions.

"What are you doing here? -- You have powers? -- Why didn't you tell me? -- Are you in our squad?"

The rapport between them was fleeting as Masai recalled the vow of detachment and silence that he made to himself. His smile fell and he moved away. Puzzled, Glacia followed.

"Masai, wait up!" He pressed forward. She overtook him. "What's the matter, Boo? Talk to me."

Masai shook his head, waving for her to go away. Glacia stopped, hurt. He never responded to her that way before.

Masai suddenly sensed foreboding movement all around him. Several Omega squad members were barreling toward him from all angles. Maffmattixx tried frantically to admonish them back, but it was too late. They were all committed now.

A knee jerk reaction, Masai steeled himself in a mask of contained fury, then -- KABOOM! A vehement wave of psychokinetic power exploded outward from him in all directions, hurling everyone dozens of meters back, their bodies smacking hard to the floor and walls.

Masai looked around savagely at the radius of Omega Squad bodies that slowly began to rouse, groggy and confused. A muscle swollen Kinetis stirred up, his movement drawing Masai's eyes to the motionless form of Glacia.

"Oh shit, what have I done?" Masai thought as he rushed over and scooped Glacia up like a new bride. Kinetis reacted, but Emosha held him back.

"Wake up, baby," Masai appealed telepathically as he shook her gently. Glacia slowly blinked open, refocusing.

"Hey, you," Glacia said with a weak but contented smile.

"You ah-ight?" Masai asked softly in her head. Glacia nodded in acknowledgement. Relieved, he placed her on her feet delicately and looked around. All eyes were on him, expressions ranging from curiosity to outright hostility. Mr. Watson's class all over again. Masai blew past everybody and marched out the door.

Masai stormed down the sector, his heart staggering in his chest. Once again, he hurt someone else with his powers that he cared for very deeply. Von Pyros suddenly appeared in front of him, stopping him in his tracks.

"I saw what you did, son. You could have killed them all. Must I remind you what your powers did to your father?"

Masai lowered his head like a scolded boy. Von Pyros then shifted gears as he regarded an approaching Glacia.

"Glacia, the beautiful Ice Empress," Von Pyros said. "How is it a goddess with such arctic powers is so full of warmth?"

Glacia looked from Von Pyros to Masai. "I can be cold when I have to be."

"I find that hard to believe," Von Pyros said as he grabbed her hand, kissing it enchantingly. "Compared to other women, you are a lily among thorns." Glacia was instantly charmed.

Masai flushed with a jealous uneasiness, an emotion he didn't know he had, had never experienced. Glacia was the only woman he ever truly cared for beyond his mother and she was his and always would be.

Cock-blocking on the low, Masai tapped Von Pyros and directed his attention to the Omega squad that were headed in their direction. Maffmattixx was leading the way, glaring at Von Pyros hard.

Von Pyros draped his arm around Masai. "Walk with me." Leading him away, Von Pyros returned to Maffmattixx a menacing stare.

"Masai," Glacia breezed out. Masai refused to acknowledge her and kept it moving. "Fine, then." She closed her eyes over tears.

The squad neared, with Axiss wearing that "I-told-you-so" look. Emosha swept her a glance as she edged close to Glacia.

"Masai's got a hidden pain," Emosha said, "And power, power unlike anything I've ever felt. He's more powerful than all of us. Combined."

Axiss almost gagged. "Him?"

"He thinks he's a chicken," Maffmattixx said.

"What?" Glacia said, annoyed.

"Masai's an eagle who thinks he's a chicken."

"You don't know him to say anything about him," Glacia said, defending her man. "Who do you think you are?" Maffmattixx trekked away. "Jerk."

TWENTY-ONE

YIELD NOT TO TEMPTATION

Von Pyros and Masai marched down a narrow hallway with Von Pyros doing all the talking.

"Let's face it," Von Pyros said, "The masses could care less about world politics or foreign relations. So the recruitment of delegates is the key in shaping the attitudes of the people."

They stopped at a door labeled, "Empyrean Killaz Music". Von Pyros opened it. Masai peeked in, humbled and curious. His eyes lit up as he beheld a state-of-the-art recording studio. Two producers were laying down a club bangin' beat at an elaborate soundboard and puffing on a blunt. Von Pyros stepped in and reached for the blunt, taking a couple of hits. He then passed the weed to Masai.

"Your talents and urban swagger would make you a treasured and celebrated entertainer the people of the world would loyally follow," Von Pyros said as he leaned a microphone close to Masai's face. "All you have to do is speak into the mic."

Masai took a slow drag on the weed as he wrestled with a decision, the influential power his words would have on listeners weighing on him heavily. Masai looked at Von Pyros intently, his face satanically ashen in his sight. He then looked from Von Pyros to the producers, their faces demoniacal.

"So what if they're devils," Masai thought. All his life he struggled with the acceptance of his divine fate and it garnered him nothing but poverty, misery and deaths of loved ones. Besides, being a rich rap superstar was something he wanted badly and couldn't hide it. He reached for the mic. Von Pyros snatched it back.

"First things first," Von Pyros said as he tugged at the belt loop of Masai's drooping pants. "Get a belt."

Over the next few days, Von Pyros insured his protégé's commitment by taking him on a whirlwind shopping spree:

At a chic men's boutique, Masai tried on several tailored outfits under Von Pyros' close supervision. He looked goth-thuggish in each one...

Bedecked with fresh glimmering jewelry, Masai cheesed as a salesperson fastened a costly watch around his wrist...

In a car dealership, Masai beamed with excitement as he revolved around a slick-red high-performance car. He hopped in and nodded to Von Pyros. This was the one…

Von Pyros led Masai through a penthouse which was decorated with stylish furniture and amenities. Masai moved past a huge fish aquarium over to the floor-to-ceiling window that opened onto a balcony. The skyline view was breathtaking. He turned to Von Pyros in disbelief.

**

Kinetis and Natasha stood in the front of the War Room as the Omega Squadron sat around a long table. A three-dimensional holograph of Johann Faust floated in the center, his extensive dossier beside it.

"Ladies and gentlemen," Kinetis said, "As you know, Johann Faust has been making extravagant threats that he and his Hands of Wrath mutants would wreak havoc on the world if anyone made a move against them and he had the means to do it. Let's examine the facts: Yesterday at oh-six hundred, the United States, in cooperation with several allied governments, performed a successful attack, taking out two-thirds of his Hands of Wrath forces. His retaliation was unconventional to say the least. Natasha?"

As Natasha spoke, the three-dimensional holograph changed to the superstructure, the "TPZ One-Thousand".

"Faust launched the TPZ One Thousand, a mass teleportation device, making an estimated thirty million people vanish from around the globe. Intel indicates that he plans to acquire global control by brainwashing those in influential positions and killing the rest. Once programmed, he plans on putting the influential individuals back in place to uproot the world as we know it, with him in power."

The image then changed to a topographical map of a Central American jungle. A lighted circle surrounded a mark and a set of coordinates on the map.

"Faust has seized a compound over the border that is owned by Embryxx Industries, holding a shitload of bigwig's hostage," Kinetis said. "Government officials, religious leaders, movie stars, girl scouts, boy scouts, you name it. This is a rescue operation of the highest order. If we don't act expeditiously, he'll have full mind-programming capability in three to six weeks. We've been ordered to deploy at oh-four hundred."

Maffmattixx jeered. "With all due respect, sir..."

"What is it, agent?" Kinetis dryly replied.

"I know I'm new around here, but this don't make sense," Maffmattixx said. "Why would Faust go through all that trouble? There are many other ways to indoctrinate people."

"And cheaper than the Turbo Tea Five Thousand," Fatal joked. Soft chuckles went through the room.

"Secure that!" Kinetis commanded. Everyone quieted down. "Your job is to preserve freedoms that others may try to usurp," Kinetis said with an edge to Maffmattixx, "So keep your opinions to yourself and just soldier. Without question."

TWENTY-TWO

THE EAGLE AND THE CHICKEN

Raunchy rap music thumped as Masai sat at a table staring at the lyrics that he scrabbled on a writing pad. Although the words were his, the context was not, comprised of an overdose of murder, money, misogyny and mayhem, ideals fathered by Von Pyros.

Masai cleared his throat then opened his mouth to rap. Nothing came out. He looked around the penthouse, hoping his appetite for opulence and fame would overpower the internal struggle between his eternal and mortal self. He tried again. Only a grunt escaped. Fuck it. He tossed the pad across the table and then began to roll himself a blunt.

A knock at the door. Masai got up, moved to it and cracked it open. Supreme Maffmattixx was standing there.

"'Sup, Fam'," Maffmattixx said. "Thought I'd come by. Make sure you not trippin'. Cats like Guerrilla… Every brother ain't a brother, 'nahmean?" Masai closed the door. Maffmattixx's foot stopped it. "Mind if I come in for a minute?"

Masai motioned him in. Maffmattixx moved through, scrutinizing the luxury high-rise. Masai sat back down, putting the finishing lick-rolls on the blunt. He offered the weed. Maffmattixx smirked, strolled over and boldly turned the music off. Masai placed the blunt behind his ear and studied Maffmattixx curiously as he became lost in the aquarium. "His third eye is closed," Maffmattixx said lowly to himself, "Forgot his teachings, who he is…"

Maffmattixx then took out a copy of the Epistles of True Wisdom and slapped it down in front of Masai.

"Seize the time." Maffmattixx then sauntered out.

A moment. Masai hadn't seen a copy of the Kindred's hallowed book since he was a child. He took a deep breath and caressed the embossed winged sun symbol on the cover in awe. Masai then thumbed through it, his mind flooding with fond tales of Kindred folklore and pedigree, reflections of a life that was no more. Between the pages were numerous photos, mostly of him in his youth with Osiris, Ashanti and the Kindred Liberation Army. There also was a note inside: "Training Room. 6 AM Sharp. Be there or be square."

Masai slammed the book shut. He took the blunt from behind his ear, sparked it, leaned back and toked.

***

Masai entered the training room, only to find Maffmattixx in the center of a boxing ring, meditating. Maffmattixx didn't lift his eyes, but he was aware of his presence.

"You're early," Maffmattixx said. "Good. Time is the one thing we can't get back so let's not waste any."

Masai climbed into the ring. Maffmattixx arose and handed him a pair of fighting mitts to put on.

"Awareness is the most pivotal aspect of telepathic combat," Maffmattixx said, tying a blindfold over Masai's eyes. "Your mind must be everywhere and nowhere at once."

Maffmattixx then slipped on punch mitts. He raised them up and began revolving around a sightless Masai.

"Where am I?"

Masai assumed a fighting stance. He sensed, lurched forward, about to swing --

"Stop!" Maffmattixx yelled. Masai lifted the blindfold. An innocent-looking old lady was cowering directly in front of him. Masai dropped his guard. Without missing a beat, the old lady clobbered him with a hook to the jaw, flattening him. Maffmattixx approached and crouched over Masai.

"You're like a point guard dribbling with your head down," Maffmattixx said. "Again."

Masai rose to his feet, re-covered his eyes and put his dukes up again. He keenly pivoted, hoofing forward. Maffmattixx stepped away, losing him. Masai bounced ahead, cocked to swing –

"Stop!" Maffmattixx yelled again. Masai lifted the blindfold. A rosy-cheeked little girl was in front of him. Her eyes quickly burned murderous as she side-kicked him across the ring. Masai fell flat on his ass, stunned.

"The governing force of telepathy is not the senses, you dig me?" Maffmattixx said, helping Masai to his feet. He then locked eyes with him and spoke very sharply. "Look within and visualize my mind in your consciousness. Again."

Masai pulled the blindfold back down and took a deep breath with a renewed meditative resolve. Maffmattixx orbited. Masai's legs somehow found their way over to him. Maffmattixx maneuvered. Masai cut the ring off. Then --

Masai located and expertly blasted away at Maffmattixx's mitts. The pace quickened. Over and over. The little girl approached from behind and swung a haymaker. Masai intuitively ducked and slammed away at her mitts. The old lady approached, swinging. Masai bobbed and countered, interchanging between all three with an impressive blind-pugilistic cadence.

***

"There are many powers that your parents had, of which you possess also," Maffmattixx said as he sat at the control booth's main console. Masai was visible on several viewport screens standing in the empty training room. Maffmattixx then shapeshifted into KLA cyberpunk Maimframe and began operating the console with the zest of a pianist. "But your true power comes from the Ether…"

The training room suddenly went black. Illumination returned and Masai was now back on the shadowy side of Mars surrounded by endless space.

"You just gotta remember, overstand that every syllable you utter has a vibration," Maimframe extolled from above, *"So when the sound of your words hit the air, matter can start to form."*

In an instant, pressurization began to decline rapidly. Masai's body levitated and his breathing began to labor. Panic set in as he heaved for air in the ultra-cold.

"Speak what you want into existence," Maimframe said.

Maimframe watched Masai squirm in agony from several viewport angles. His face began to puff and his eyes bulged from decompression. Maimframe immediately shut down the holographic cosmos, returning the training room to normal.

Masai gasped heavily as his body lowered to the floor, his features and oxygen gradually returning to him. Maimframe migrated over, transforming back into Maffmattixx on the move. He helped Masai to his feet.

"A tortured soul cannot fulfill a destiny."

Masai shrugged free, his anger falling on Maffmattixx.

"You're supposed to be fit for the company of Gods, but you'd rather stay mentally castrated on some mortal shit!"

Masai shouldered past. Maffmattixx shadowed him.

"Oh, my bad," Maffmattixx said, "You're the eagle that was raised in a chicken coop." Masai registered the remark but kept walking. "Yeah, that's it. You've got an eagle's genes, history and power, but you think you're a chicken."

Masai stalked to the exit, trying to restrain himself. Maffmattixx didn't let up, driving the words hard.

"You dream chicken dreams, think chicken thoughts... I'll bet your greatest goal in life is to be more like the chickens. Well, let me give you the skinney. You may have forgotten who you are, but that jive-dude Von Pyros didn't. He knows if you ever realized --"

That's it. Masai turned to punch -- CLAP! Maffmattixx caught his fist. A tense, muscle-bulging moment between them.

"I'm an eagle, swooping down from the stratosphere..." Maffmattixx then shapeshifted into Ashanti.

"Masai... We don't have much time."

Masai withdrew his hand as he stared into his mother's face, confused as he'd ever been. He then turned and stormed out. Maffmattixx reverted to himself and just stood there in the center of the room, drained.

***

In Empyrean Killaz recording studio, Masai stood in the sound booth wearing headphones, mechanically bobbing his head to an aggressive beat. He looked cool on the outside, but on the inside, he was shook.

Masai leaned into the microphone, seemingly humbled by its presence. With a spurt of surging will, he found his voice and began releasing the anxiety that welled up inside him with a palpable rhythmic power. The producers exchanged knowing smiles.

***

Masai was alone in the gym putting on a basketball clinic. Each spectacular move was an expression of his fluctuating emotions: Anger. Doubt. Fear. The ball rolled out of bounds and stopped under an icy-scythed stiletto.

"Still got the moves," Glacia said, her foot on the ball. Masai was so enraptured in his own thoughts that he hadn't noticed the click-clack of her heels approaching. He snatched the ball from under her foot and resumed shooting.

"Just got our orders," Glacia said. "Going out at dawn. Thought you should know."

Masai crisply sank a jump shot, disregarding her.

"I've been thinking about something for quite a while," Glacia said as she moved in closer. "I don't know what to do. I was wondering if you could help me."

Masai retrieved the ball and looked at her quizzically. Glacia stepped in front of him with a sexy pout, her eyes raw and sexual. "I think you know what."

Glacia leaned in to kiss him. Masai pulled away. She grabbed his face and looked deep into his eyes, searching.

"When you look in the mirror, do you see the same man that I see?" Masai snatched his face away, an awkward sense of shame. "Guess not."

Glacia shouldered past and headed out. Masai reached for her, but it was too late. He hurled the ball in frustration.

TWENTY-THREE

Spellbound

"And here in our Philadelphia studio, a rare sit-down with multi-business tycoon, philanthropist and newly appointed global ambassador, Dorian Von Pyros,"* reporter Jordyn Martinez said as the television camera held tight on her in a close-up. *"Mr. Von Pyros, thanks for taking the time out of your busy schedule."*

The camera pulled back, revealing Von Pyros sitting across from her, a "WPHZ News" placard forming the backdrop.

"Call me Dorian, Jordyn," Von Pyros said. *"And may I say your sparkling eyes capture my soul every time I visit this city."*

"Thank you, um, Dorian, yes," Jordyn blushed, then quickly jumped back into seasoned media poise. *"After the disappearances, the shocking announcement was made that you've been recognized as the only legitimate representative between the mutants and world leaders and that a breakthrough was imminent. How did that come about?"*

"I quietly made contact with emissaries on both sides through a friendly government, contending that peace can only be achieved through compromise."

"But why you?" Jordyn asked. *"Why were you successful and others were not?"*

"Sincerity, Integrity," Von Pyros said. *"And as an old friend once said, 'real recognize real'."*

"What about the millions who have vanished from the planet?" Jordyn said. *"Some have speculated --"*

"I cannot disclose any information at this time," Von Pyros interjected, *"But we know the mu-terrorists responsible. It will not go unpunished."*

Jordyn kept up the pressure. *"What about the internet rumors that you're a demagogue, that you subvert governments and snatch elections, your use of the media, ties with mob bosses..."*

"That's funny," Von Pyros grinned. *"Powerful men have always been painted formidably, horrific images of the few controlling the many. I've given untold millions to famine, stem cell research, space travel... Are these the actions of a devil?"*

"Uh no, well no."

"That is why tomorrow," Von Pyros said, *"Here in the City of Brotherly Love, the world will see something totally unprecedented, the signing of the Global Peace Covenant. As God is my witness, I will do whatever is necessary to make this world a safe place for Mankind --"*

The scene flicked away and pulled back, revealing a television screen. Across from the TV, Axiss was channel-surfing with the remote in her bedroom, careful not to tarnish her freshly polished fingernails. She finally settled on a pseudo-reality show where a bevy of lively divas were poppin' bottles in the back of a limousine.

"Y'all bitches is lit!" Axiss exclaimed to the TV as she shook her wrists limply to dry her nails.

Suddenly, an ominous fog began to enshroud the room. It seemed almost alive. Axiss stopped moving and looked around, befuddled. Then through the diminishing fog, a figure moved to her, sauntering over with the silky smoothness of a finesse pimp. It was Von Pyros.

"Come with me and I will bathe you in the finest gold on earth, woven with exotic jewels from other worlds."

Axiss was spellbound.

TWENTY-FOUR

OPERATION: TRIPLE-SIX

Several members of the Omega Squad were in the armory strapping on their sleek combat gear like they were getting ready for the big game, complete with emblazoned Omega Squadron outfits, body armor and headsets.

"Why must I wear this awful device?" Mister Mystiqal said, dropping his headset in frustration. "It hinders my arcane perceptions." Earth Angel picked up the headset and adjusted it for him like a dutiful spouse.

"You know how Kinetis is," Earth Angel said. "He's a by-the-book kind of guy. Besides, even at half power, you're still the greatest mystic the world has ever seen."

"Earth Angel my friend," Mister Mystiqal said, "You have never been mistaken."

Their attentions suddenly angled over to Hoodrat, who was shamelessly stripping butt-ass naked as she suited up. Her shapely frame also garnered a stare from Kid Hardkore, who was tattooing a rocket launcher on Fatal's shoulder. Distracted, Hardkore pricked Fatal with the needle.

"Ow!" Fatal yelled. "Yo, man, pay attention!"

"My bad, dawg," Hardkore grinned. "Stop bitchin'."

As Hardkore wiped the blood away, his eyes followed Glacia as she stepped in with a distressed look on her face. She made her way over to her locker and started to break down, the enormity of her emotions hitting her. Hardkore moved to her, concerned. "Are you alright?"

Glacia looked away, fighting back tears. "I think I just have the right love at the wrong time."

Hardkore swallowed hard, preparing to express the puppy love that burned in his heart. "Dude is a nut. He doesn't even deserve a woman like you, someone who is as beautiful on the inside as she is on the outside. If you were my girl, I'd treat you like the princess... no, no, the queen that you are."

"Thanks, Corey," Glacia said, giving him a chummy hug. "You're a very good friend." She then turned and began fishing around in her locker.

Hardkore stood there a moment, his hopes of reciprocated adoration crushed. Banished to the dreaded "friend zone", he took that long walk back over to a snickering Fatal.

***

Bedecked in sleek emblazoned outfits, the motley crew of super-commandos climbed aboard a huge transport chamber which was beyond hi-tech, lined with seats. The last members to board, Johnny Fatal and Kid Hardkore, prowled the aisle with a streetwise bravado and "wet behind the ears" machismo.

"This ain't no video game." Kataklysmo said. "This is the real deal."

"I ain't worried about nothin', yo," Fatal said, lifting his shirt to reveal his tatted arsenal of weapons, vehicles and explosives. "I'm state of the art."

Emosha yanked Fatal and pulled him into a seat beside her while Hardkore planted himself next to Glacia.

In the command seat, Kinetis flicked a few switches. A low rumble began to vibrate the chamber just as Shadowstar and Skizzo climbed aboard.

"In lieu of Axiss' sudden illness, we've got a couple of late additions here to assist. Shadowstar and Skizzo," Kinetis said.

Groans parroted around. Emosha's eyes fixed on them as they took a seat, their auras creating within her an instant animosity. She then gave a disapproving glance to Kinetis.

"Orders," Kinetis said. "Don't ask."

Emosha brandished a dagger and masterfully twirled it between her fingers as she eyed them coldly.

"Initiate teleportation sequencer on my mark," Kinetis said into his headset. "Three. Two. One. Mark!"

The feeling of increased acceleration was monstrous as their bodies disappeared from the transport chamber and concentered into a blinding flash of light --

-- Shafts of daylight filtered through the tropical mosaic of green as exotic sounds echoed across the Central American rainforest. A sudden breach slashed across the sky just above treetop level. The Omega squad actualized out of it, crashed through the umbrella of trees and hit the ground running...

***

In the ritual room of a nearby facility in the jungle, the Brotherhood of the Vampyrian czars encircled a large glass cylinder with a semi-nude **CLONE OF VON PYROS** inside.

The real Von Pyros, dressed in ceremonial regalia, stepped out of the shadows grandly. He opened his robe, his all-seeing eye blinking in the center of his chest.

"Cell of the Son of Perdition," Von Pyros bellowed, "Awaken and lead the forces of Hell into eternity!"

Von Pyros beamed with a sick glee as quantities of entities emerged from his chest-eye and penetrated the clone. The Clone then opened its eyes and released an accursed breath that passed through the room and across all the waters of Central America...

TWENTY-FIVE

EMBRYXX INDUSTRIES

Emosha whacked through the jungle's dense brush with her photon sword, followed by the rest of the team in a solemn procession. Feeling an ominous shift in the atmosphere, Emosha halted at a clearing just as a flock of birds exploded across the sky in a fright. The rest of the Omega Squad assumed defensive positions as the Clone's foreboding breath breezed through them like the chill of an icy wind.

Kinetis hand signaled. Hoodrat dutifully scampered up a tree with vermin-like dexterity. Kinetis then moved alongside Emosha, who was sweeping the locale with her sword, analyzing the rainforest's ecosystem.

"What is it?" Kinetis whispered as he scanned from tree line to terrain all around. Emosha didn't respond as she stayed locked in investigation with her highly sensitive emotions and various electromagnetic optical ranges. But none of her talents gave her an explanation for the impalpable distress that was wasting away.

"Nothing," Emosha said dismissively. Following her cue, everyone began to breathe easy except Earth Angel. He was visibly more neurotic than the others.

"You alright?" Glacia asked.

"Y-Yeah," Earth Angel muttered as he ran his hand nervily through his hair. "I think."

"I'll bet he pissed his panties," Guerrilla said.

Ever the hardened professional, Kinetis stepped in front of the team and struck a pose, chest out, fists on hips.

"Alright, stay sharp, people. Let's grab the hostages and go home. First squad up."

Under Kinetis' direction, the team of Guerrilla, Shadowstar and Skizzo advanced through the thick foliage to Embryxx Industries so quietly that you could hear an ant piss on cotton.

***

Kindred markings crudely embellished the three-building compound of Embryxx Industries in the middle of seclusion. Two Hands of Wrath sentries patrolled the exterior front of the main building, while a third occupied the front desk inside.

Noticing a slight movement in the darkness of the foliage, one sentry signaled the other and they both moved cautiously toward the shady brush --

Shadowstar sprang out of the shadows at them, shadowsword in hand. He sliced the first across the throat with fatal precision. The other sentry swung a sword that crackled with energy. Shadowstar blocked it with his sword, his free hand deftly drawing another sword from a shadow and in the same motion, slashed him across the midsection, disemboweling him.

Ogling the butchery outdoors, the desk sentry flew out of the main entrance on arthropodic wings. Shadowstar threw a dart into his neck in mid-draw of his gat, killing him.

Shadowstar then jetted inside of the main building and placed a sticky bomb with a detonation timer under the front desk. It read 00:59:59 and was counting down.

"I'm in," Shadowstar said into his headset. Guerrilla and Skizzo scampered out of the darkness and raced into the building with Shadowstar.

"Third squad," Kinetis said, "Hold your position here on the perimeter. Second squad, let's move."

With Emosha at point, the second team of Kinetis, Glacia, Mister Mystiqal and an uneasy Earth Angel moved through the heavy foliage towards Embryxx Industries.

***

In his Embryxx Industries office, Dr. Tucci sat on the floor cradling an almost empty bottle of Hennessy. His five-o'clock shadow was turning six-thirty and he looked as if he slept in his clothes.

"I never truly believed in you before," Tucci slurred as he appealed to the ceiling. "Not sure if I do now..."

In an Embryxx building bathroom, Skizzo split into two as the duo skulked up behind a Hands of Wrath guard taking a piss.

A Skizzo snapped the guard's neck while the other affixed a sticky bomb under the urinal...

"If you're out there listening," Tucci beseeched, "Wrath the Conqueror... please forgive me, protect me..."

In a vast medical lab, a burly Hands of Wrath guard entered the medical lab to an eerie stillness. She moved past a dozen specimen-filled cylinders, her shotgun at the ready. Sensing a presence behind her, she whirled, her arms poised to fire -- her leader and comrade Johann Faust was there, fearfully protesting by waving both hands. She relented.

A strange shit-eating grin suddenly took over Faust's face as his fists charged with fission energy -- KA-BLAMM! Faust fired on her with an atomic blast. For a brief instant, her body looked like it was caught in an X-ray as the blast punched a frying pan-sized hole through her torso, continuing through to the wall behind...

"I'll do whatever I can to fix things," Tucci said, taking a swig from the bottle. "I promise. Just don't let me die..."

A deathly thud suddenly came from outside of the office. Tucci scrambled behind his desk, reached inside a drawer and pulled out a handgun.

"Faust?" Tucci called as he shakily aimed the gun at the door. "Is that you?"

The door exploded open and the Skizzos plodded in, consuming the room. Tucci opened fire. Slugs sparked off their durable structures as he emptied his clip in dismay.

Shadowstar entered from a shadow within the room. He affixed a sticky bomb to a lampshade and the fearsome triplet then loomed in formidably. Tucci was scared shitless.

"I'm not gonna say anything," Tucci groveled as the gun slipped out of his hand. A Skizzo tossed the desk aside effortlessly. It burst into splinters against the wall. "I'm not gonna say anything...Oh God...please, NO... NNOOOO!!!!"

Outside of the main building, Tucci crashed through the window in an explosion of glass. His limbs flailed wildly as he plunged several stories to his death.

TWENTY-SIX

APOCRYPHA

Kinetis, Emosha, Glacia, Mister Mystiqal and Earth Angel emerged on a hill and took cover behind a heavy patch of leafage above Embryxx Industries.

"Looks quiet," Earth Angel said lowly.

"That's the illusion they want you to see," Kinetis said. He then belly-crawled a few meters to the edge of the knoll and swept the complex with his thermoscopic eye:

Four dead bodies on the ground. Numerous fresh kills throughout the complex, the glowing-red heat from their bodies fading to black.

Grim-faced, Kinetis hand-signaled his squad into action. Mister Mystiqal soared high atop the compound for aerial surveillance. Everyone else bolted toward Embryxx Industries. Bending the light around her, Emosha vanished on the move.

***

Kinetis moved down the center building's corridor. He approached a medical wing door and pushed it open --

Devastation. Several lab-coated bodies carpeted the floor. Blood splatter bedecked the walls. Spider-webbed cracks surrounded a crater in the wall where a body was vehemently hurled into it.

"Emosha," Kinetis said into his headset, "Anything?"

In the rear building's corridor, Emosha became visible as she stood over a Hands of Wrath guard's body, his throat slit. "Nothing," Emosha replied, "But death."

"I know what you mean," Kinetis' voice said. "Meet me in Operations in the main building."

***

In the main building's top floor, Glacia entered the medical lab, the pale neon glow of stasis cylinders exacerbating the spookiness. Moving toward the cylinders, she gave a cursory glance to the corrosive hole in the wall as she stepped past the Hands of Wrath guard's cauterized torso.

Inside of the cylinders, grisly humanoid specimens floated in a murky amniotic fluid, their twisted translucid skin making it difficult to tell where one body part began and another ended. Glacia's face contorted in repulsion as she gazed upon a live specimen swishing in one of the tanks, its eyes and mouth hideously misshapen in excruciating agony. She then grabbed a folder from atop of its cylinder and thumbed through it.

In an adjacent room, unique mainframe computers and cabinets framed the room with robots and prosthetics suspended all around. Earth Angel quietly entered and moved through nervily, looking back often. He glanced over and saw Glacia absorbed in a folder. Moving to her, he bumped into a prosthetic that clanged another, causing a chain reaction, startling Glacia.

"Sorry," Earth Angel said as he gracelessly tried to stop them from swinging. Glacia resumed her preoccupation with the file. "The subject's name is Vampyro."

Earth Angel looked at her quizzically as he approached.

"You've heard of him?" Glacia asked.

"Vampyro was one of the fallen angels that fell to earth with Lucifer," Earth Angel said. "Supposedly he was his most loyal and bloodthirsty servant."

"That sounds crazy," Glacia said.

"Just bear with me," Earth Angel said. "According to legend, Vampyro and the fallen angels mated with earth women and had kids. This hybrid bloodline became the illumed 'Brotherhood of the Vampyrians', with an agenda of world domination. Some say they still walk the earth today."

"Where'd you hear about this?" Glacia inquired.

"Spent three years at Seminary," Earth Angel said. "Kinda was the family business."

"This log was last checked a week ago by an Aries Tucker," Glacia said, reading the handwritten entries on a chart printout. "The case history spans two decades. Apparently, they've tried to clone this Vampyro hundreds of times and now it's completed."

***

In Operations directly below the med lab, Emosha was navigating through a computer database. Kinetis walked in, his forehead pleated with confusion.

"No missing people anywhere," Kinetis said. "But there's over a dozen scientists and several notorious mutant fugitives, all dead. Just what the hell are we doing here?"

"I'm taking an interest in precious metals," Emosha said. "Tucci apparently did. All of the major refineries worldwide have merged into a company called Empyrean Ventures."

"You think there's a link between Empyrean Ventures and the disappearances somehow?" Kinetis asked.

"Not sure, but I found something interesting," Emosha said as she punched keys non-stop. "An existing company with a similar name, Empyrean Investors. So I ran a personnel retrieval on Empyrean Investors and it's a ghost, a dummy corporation. No directors, no employees, just a website with a CEO listed. Someone by the name of Aries Tucker."

"Sounds like someone's been tricking financiers into thinking they're buying shares in Empyrean Ventures but are really investing in Empyrean Investors," Kinetis said.

"And Tucci knew it," Emosha said as Aries' photo and dossier popped up on the screen. "Aries is an expert weapons combatant, can generate any weapon and charge it with highly explosive biokinetic energy on impact...organic crimson armor...undercover operative in the Kindred Liberation

Army...credited with the assassination of KLA chairwoman Ashanti Jackson during Operation Empyrean Serpent..."

Kinetis' jaw set grimly as he mentally processed the events of Operation Empyrean Serpent and the present mission, culminating in his dreaded epiphany.

"This wasn't a rescue operation," Kinetis said. "We were chaperoning assassins in. This was a hit."

TWENTY-SEVEN

VAMPYRIAN ACTIVITY

In the jungle, Hoodrat scampered high into the treetops across branches and vines. She bounded onto a thick tree limb in a motionless crouch, her amplified senses on high alert. The light breeze through the leaves magnified in her ears like a gale-force wind blowing through a small town. Through the leafy curtain of an adjacent tree, a tarantula feasting upon a beetle sounded to her like a lion tearing into a gazelle carcass.

Breathing easy, Hoodrat reached through the thicket and plucked a piece of colorful fruit. She bit into the produce heartily, its thirst-quenching juices snaking down her face. She suddenly stopped in mid-chomp and sniffed the suffocating air. Her face twisted in revulsion. She then emerged from a tree and joined up with her team of Supreme Maffmattixxx, Johnny Fatal, Kid Hardkore and Kataklysmo, who were assembled at a clearing.

"Y'all smell that?" Hoodrat asked.

"You're the one with the heightened sense of smell," Kid Hardkore said as he breathed in, detecting nothing. "What does it smell like?"

"Like rotten eggs," Hoodrat said.

"Probably just a skunk," Kataklysmo said as he swatted at the ants that bit at him steadily.

"Or her pussy," Fatal gibed. Hoodrat gave him the finger.

"It's sulfur," Maffmattixx said as he panned around, stopping at a deep-walled canyon a half-mile away. "And only one thing gives off that jacked-up smell when it enters our dimension..." Everyone followed his gaze...

Near the canyon, obscure blotched outlines were gradually coming into being, forming into a legion of undead-like creatures of seemingly fierce hunger and unfathomable terror. Their rotting skin had rupturing boils that made a perpetual popping sound and their fangs and talons seemed to exist for one thing: tearing flesh.

Maffmattixx's face wrenched with horror. "Vampyrians."

With a bone-chilling screech from the presumed leader, the Vampyrians began accelerating slowly into a skittering, predatory run toward them.

Maffmattixx quickly played quarterback. "I'll take point. Kataklysmo, Hoodrat. Flanking positions. Kid Hardkore, Johnny Fatal --"

All heads turned to see Fatal running away at top speed. Everyone looked at the creatures. Then at each other. All bravado lost. They ran after Fatal…

***

"Every KLA affiliation that Aries has had is in this folder," Emosha said as a perpetual stream of Kindred names whizzed down the computer screens.

"Let me see something," Kinetis said as he leaned in and typed S-u-p-r-e-m-e M-a-f-f-m-a-t-t-i-x-x. Maffmatixx's KLA dossier appeared. "I knew it."

Kinetis raised his metal fist -- TCHIKK! An elongated strip of metal jutted out from between his knuckles. He inserted the strip into the computer's USB port, copying its infinite data. Kinetis then went back to the root folder and resumed scrolling.

"Wait!" Emosha said tensely. "Back up."

Kinetis scrolled back slowly, stopping at his own pseudonym within the Kindred archive. "What the hell…? I'm not a Kindred."

A brief look flowed between them. Kinetis then scrolled back through the lexicon of names, gliding by Hoodrat, then Guerrilla, then Glacia…

"Here you are," Kinetis said, clicking on Emosha's dossier. "Emosha, age twenty-eight, superior martial artist, powers based on light --"

"Turn it off!" Emosha shrieked, throwing herself at the computer. Kinetis easily immobilized her with his beefy arm. She thrashed about, maneuvering into his lap wildly but purposely. "Retrieves photonic weapons from an invisible pocket dimension…"

In the naughty ruckus, the computer's cursor staggered back and forth, flashing back to the database of names. "Can manipulate others' emotions but can't …wait, just a second…"

Then, a haunting click of the computer. Emosha's eyes strayed back to the screen and stared at the extensive dossier that was now before her.

"Masai Jackson, age twenty-two," Emosha said as she re-took her seat. She looked on in awe at the plethora of classified information on Masai; from the supernatural capabilities that resided within his earthly vessel, to his relationship with surrogate father figure Stanley and to his early beginnings with his parents and the KLA.

Emosha tracked her fingers down the screen at the genealogical listing that seemed to be endless. "Parents, grandparents, great-great-great grandparents… His lineage traced so far back. Why?"

***

Mister Mystiqal hovered high in the exterior of the main building, fiddling with his headset in frustration. Unbeknownst to him, Faust was on the rooftop of an adjacent building, taking aim at him with his nuclear-imbued fists. Fed up with the headset, Mystiqal threw it down to the ground. He suddenly whirled to Faust, his eyes wide with terror…

***

175

"We'd better tell the others about this Vampyro cloning thing," Glacia said to Earth Angel. "Kinetis, you read me? Come in, over... Mystiqal, what's your position? Emosha... Our link is cut off."

"That's the least of our worries," Earth Angel said. Glacia followed his look. An explosive charge was affixed to a glass cylinder with the readout displaying 00:08:11 and counting down. As if psychically connected, the twosome then made a beeline toward the exit.

Sensing a sudden change in the air pattern, Earth Angel lunged, tackling Glacia to the floor -- a flailing Mister Mystiqal burst through the wall overhead, dangerously close. He crashed through several prosthetics and cylinders and slammed against the opposite wall, knocked out. Specimens sloshed to the floor amid gelatinous matter and glass.

Trivial amounts of out sweepings blanketed Glacia and Earth Angel. They looked over and saw Faust standing just inside the new entryway, smoke dispensing from his hands...

***

"What the hell was that?" Kinetis said to the ceiling as he retracted his metal strip from the computer. Emosha turned in time to see Shadowstar step out of a shadow on the wall, a shadowspear in his grasp. She drew her sword. "Game time."

TWENTY-EIGHT

GUERRILLA WARFARE

Johann Faust's fists geared up for another atom-smashing energy burst just as Earth Angel and Glacia sprang up and assumed a battle posture. Fully charged, Faust beamed an atomic blast --

KA-BOOM! Earth Angel and Glacia lunged out of the way as a huge hole was corrosively blown in the wall just inches from where they were standing. Earth Angel popped up and returned a shot of concussive air --

-- Guerrilla surprisingly leaped out of Faust's body just as Faust was whammed, propelling him out of the building, into a tree and plummeting eight fatal stories to the ground.

Glacia moved like lightning and began assailing Guerrilla with a furious kicking assault, her ice-razored stilettos leaving a vaporous trail as they cleaved through the air. Guerrilla expertly dodged as the heels whizzed by, barely missing his face. Spotting an opening, he lurched forward and slammed into her, phasing inside of her body.

Glacia/Guerrilla whirled and flung an icicle-etched playing card at Earth Angel, clipping him in the shoulder. Earth Angel dropped, wincing in pain. Guerrilla then stepped out of Glacia and backhanded her to the floor.

"Always knew sooner or later I was gonna get inside you," Guerrilla said, grinning like a psycho. He then leveled his gun at her, her eyes wide with terror...

A live specimen suddenly bound up behind Guerrilla with a ghastly hiss. He spun around just as it swung what looked like the beginnings of a talon, smacking him hard to the wall.

Glacia quickly shot the specimen with an arctic blast that spread artery-like through its body, freezing it. She then kicked it to smithereens, ice chips exploding everywhere -- Earth Angel gestured, his wind power re-directing the ice at Guerrilla. Guerrilla evaded and took cover behind a metal cabinet as the ice splatted against the sheet rock...

On the floor below, the door was suddenly knocked off its hinges and Skizzo rushed through, plowing over to Kinetis like an express train. Skizzo landed several thunderous punches that inflated Kinetis' physical structure and passions.

Kinetis finally exploded with a hook to the jaw, the impact knocking Skizzo past Emosha and Shadowstar, who were engaged in a vehement dance of combat. Their martial arts mastery was on full display as their weapons clanged in broken staccato rhythms, their skill level, equivalent.

Skizzo got to his feet, a burst of fiery energy suddenly flaring around his fists. He replicated another Skizzo and the duo flanked Kinetis perilously. One Skizzo maneuvered Kinetis into a full-nelson while the other molly-hopped him with haymakers, the energy doing excruciating damage.

Swollen with power, Kinetis clutched the fingers of the Skizzo behind him, forcing him to release his grip. He slung him to the ground and stomped him fatally. Kinetis then seized the other Skizzo one-handed by the neck, snapped it and hurled him through the ceiling --

Amid falling plaster, an unconscious Mister Mystiqal crashed down and collapsed into the room like a rag doll. Emosha instinctively turned to her fallen comrade -- Shadowstar wheeled a kick to her face and assaulted her with a barrage of wallops that sent her reeling...

"Get down to Operations!" Earth Angel yelled to Glacia as he kept Guerrilla at bay behind the cabinet with air blasts. Glacia dutifully somersaulted through the hole to the floor below.

Huddled behind the cabinet and fisting two pistols, Guerrillla glanced at his watch: 00:02:13... 00:02:12... 00:02:11... He then looked desperately around the med lab, zeroing in on the huge cavity in the wall that Mister Mystiqal had crashed through.

In an anxious burst of fear and fury, Guerrilla pushed the cabinet over and startled Earth Angel, who recoiled a split second, which was just enough time for him to tuck, roll and

179

come up firing. Earth Angel barely leaped out of the way as the bullets shattered cylinders, turning the med lab into a rainstorm of glass, fluid and grisly flesh. Guerrilla lunged toward the hole in the wall just as Earth Angel dove through the hole in the floor --

-- Earth Angel's wings expanded as he whisked through Operations and punched Shadowstar, wobbling him. Shadowstar then rolled into a shadow on the wall and disappeared, a head-hunting ice-card piercing through the wall a hair behind him.

"The whole building's about to blow any second!" Glacia said, anxiety thick in her voice.

"Mission compromised!" Kinetis yelled as he helped a woozy Mystiqal to his feet. "Abort!"

"The extraction point is ten klicks away," Mystiqal said weakly. "We gotta go!" Kinetis screamed in his face, "Now!"

Mystiqal gestured and generated a magical tempest that clouded the room. The storm abated, dissipated and the Omega Squadron was gone.

00:00:02... 00:00:01... 00:00:00. KA-BLAMM!! A series of staggered explosions hurtled matter into the air as the Embryxx Industries complex mushroomed and collapsed in the jungle.

TWENTY-NINE

KEEPIN' IT HARDKORE

The Embryxx Industries' series of explosions quaked the terrain with deafening roars, jarring Kid Hardkore, Supreme Maffmattixx, Hoodrat and Kataklysmo off their feet. Having discarded their armor and headsets, they quickly recovered and kept a breakneck pace through the jungle with Hardkore pulling away and Kataklysmo bringing up the rear.

Exhausted, Kataklysmo stopped and rested his hands on his knees. Hoodrat doubled back and grabbed his arm, pulling him. Kataklysmo jerked free.

"I'll hold them off," Kataklysmo said, forcing steadiness into words through heavy breathing. Feeding off his fear, Hoodrat started to whimper.

"I'll catch up," Kataklysmo said, "Promise..." Hoodrat reluctantly gathered herself and scurried down an embankment.

Kataklysmo stood fully as Vampyrians began to close in, engulfing his peripheral. He shut his eyes and inhaled, summoning all his eruptive energy in a frozen moment of hesitation, creatures upon him --

KA-BOOM! Maffmattixx and Hoodrat stumbled from the seismic blast as the top of the mound flashed brilliantly. Demonic shrills receded as the duo slowed to a stop. Hoodrat turned to Maffmattixx with trepidation.

"You think 'Klysmo got 'em all?"

"Look."

A soul-twisting nightmare. Vampyrians seemingly grew out of the horizon of the hill, their fiendish screeches commencing again with renewed fervor.

And they're off! Maffmattixx and Hoodrat bolted through the underbrush, the Vampyrians hot on their heels.

Maffmattixx stretched out his hand on the fly. Electromagnetic waves rippled, creating a portal ahead of them. "With me!"

Maffmattixx raced through the time-streaming abyss with Hoodrat following behind. The portal burst into nothingness and the Vampyrians raced onward maniacally...

***

Johnny Fatal was running for his life through the jungle's thicket, a wild desperate look on his face. He skidded, tumbled down a steep slope and hit the bottom. Threw his headset and body armor to the ground. Snatched a tattoo from his abdomen. It expanded into a sleek hovercycle. Fatal climbed on. VRROOOM! He was out.

Kid Hardkore made it down the slope and had Fatal's cloudy trail of dust and gravel in his sight. With his powerful legs and endurance, Hardkore picked up speed, caught up with him at a clearing and ran alongside.

"Why are you runnin'?" Hardkore said.

"I ain't never seen nothin' like those things in real life, yo," Fatal said. "Why are you runnin'?"

"We runnin' 'cuz you runnin'!"

Fatal and Hardkore were in overdrive as they streaked through a hair-pin gap between two branches. Hardkore stopped at the edge of a clearing and looked back. The Vampyrians were gaining. Narrowing the gap. Closing in on their prey.

"Nix this." With his back to the creatures, Kid Hardkore blindly threw a haymaker punch. The closest Vampyrian ran into it head-on, dropping dead in its tracks. Hardkore fearlessly went headlong into the legion and swung in every direction, smashing Vampyrian bones as if they were glass. He grabbed a large Vampyrian and suplexed it, breaking its back. A second wave of Vampyrians dogpiled on top of him. Hardkore let out an excruciating scream as they gnashed hungrily into his rugged flesh.

Fatal sucked up his fear and raced back, ripping a tatted Uzi from his cheek. "Get off my dawg!" Fatal streaked by and fired upon the Vampyrians that were on top of Hardkore, pumping his courage up with rants of swearing. He made a deft u-turn around a tree and proceeded to riddle them again in a murderous frenzy.

A Vampyrian leaped toward Fatal from above, its salivating jaws stretching wide -- a second Vampyrian tackled the first in mid-leap and promptly ravaged it to death. Petrified, Fatal watched as the triumphant Vampyrian began to shapeshift into -- Supreme Maffmattixx.

With a wink, Maffmattixx shapeshifted into his former ally Aries and jumped into the fray, his interchanging weapon bludgeoning and cutting creatures down in their tracks.

Hoodrat and ten of her off springs suddenly sprang out of the trees. They swooped down on the Vampyrians that were on top of Hardkore and began clawing and biting into them with feral abandon. Hardkore emerged from the deluge, weary, bleeding, but still firing devastating blows.

A Vampyrian flanked in and raked Hardkore across the thigh, striping him with deep lacerations. Hardkore grimaced as the Vampyrian lunged, tackling him. The thing drew back its claws, set to deliver the killing blow --

-- Suddenly, the Vampyrian's head catapulted back as an icicle-etched playing card, the "Jack of Diamond", pierced surgically through its forehead. The "Queen of Spade" zinged right behind it, penetrating its chest. Hardkore blearily looked off, roughly a hundred meters in the direction from where the cards came from --

"Pinochle," Glacia said as she stood at the lip of an immense portal that floated about a meter above the ground. Kinetis, Emosha and Earth Angel flanked Glacia and behind them, Mister Mystiqal's outstretched hands tensed mightily as he struggled to hold the portal open with his mystic power.

"Emergency evac!" Kinetis barked as he stomped down, rumbling a shockwave that dropped dozens of creatures. "Earth Angel, aerial assault! Emosha, clear a path! Glacia, get the Kid!"

Earth Angel gestured as he flapped into the air. Jungle vines amazingly came alive and ensnared fallen beasts. He then picked off creatures with condensed pockets of wind, sending them flying.

Emosha turned invisible and went on an imperceptible killing spree, swashbuckling through scores of Vampyrians. Glacia followed her path and arctic blasted, turning onrushing demons into horrendous frozen statues.

Glacia arrived at a battle-weary Kid Hardkore. She bolstered him up just as an undersized Vampyrian scurried toward them, ferret quick. It leaped -- Glacia spun and delivered a perfectly timed kick, her icy-scythed heel cleaving through the creature's chest. She snatched her foot and the thing dropped like a bad habit.

"I love you, Glacia." She acknowledged Hardkore with a half-smile as two Hoodrats arrived and took him from her. They draped his arms over their shoulders and the trio stumbled toward the portal. Glacia then joined her Omega offensive line as they steamrolled their way through the red zone of the satanic defense.

Battle cries and demonic shrieks echoed in the jungle air as the Omega Squad scrapped bravely. But there were too many to fend off. The Kinetis/Hoodrat went down. Then another three Hoodrats were mortally wounded. Four more were ravaged to death.

Johnny Fatal raced beyond the portal and fish-tailed his hovercycle to a slick stop. In a kamikaze charge, he gunned his cycle toward a mob that was closing in on Hardkore and the Hoodrats. Just before impact, Fatal vaulted backwards off the bike, acrobatically rolled into the portal and fired at the onrushing hovercycle. It exploded, engulfing a major bulk of the creatures squealing in flames.

Fatal moved alongside Mystiqal, whose face was a mask of strained concentration as he struggled to keep the portal open with every bit of strength in his soul.

"Hurry up, yo!" Fatal yelled, laying down a curtain of cover fire. "Mystiqal can't hold the portal open much longer!"

Earth Angel scooped Glacia and Emosha on the fly and sailed into the portal. As the trio touched down, Mystiqal stiffly went down on one knee. His hold was slipping and the portal was beginning to constrict. They promptly joined Fatal in firing long range, with Emosha flinging photon stars.

Maffmatixx teleported in with Hoodrat. He instantly shapeshifted into Torchure and began discharging blasts of fire, char-broiling the last bit of pursuing beasts.

Cemetery silence. Bonfires flickered across the shredded jungle that was layered with scores of dead Vampyrians. A battered Kid Hardkore grimaced in pain as the two Hoodrats hobbled him up to the gateway, which was about seven feet aboveground due to the constricting of it. Kinetis took Hardkore and hoisted him up to a reaching Fatal, who was on the edge of weeping. "I gotchu, dawg..."

Suddenly, a camouflaged Vampyrian materialized in mid-flight and seized Hardkore from Kinetis' grasp, driving him to the ground. Fatal and Kinetis both fell back, startled.

Dozens more Vampyrians materialized and assailed Kinetis and the two Hoodrats, plunging them down under the cacophony of gnashing and growling that had besieged Hardkore. Everyone that was capable of firing distance attacks opened up.

A metallic hand abruptly crept up through the Vampyrian mound. With an indomitable will and muscles on top of muscles, Kinetis climbed out of the deluge, flinging Vampyrians off him as if they were a pack of wild rats. He banged two Vampyrian heads together lethally then dove headfirst through the narrowing portal.

Then, with an overexerted groan, Mystiqal collapsed and the portal began to close rapidly. Maffmattixx pulled a mad-firing Fatal back just before the portal could choke on his arms. He broke free and charged forward, irrational and hysterical.

"It's a wrap!" Maffmattixx yelled, laying controlling hands on Fatal's shoulders. "He's gone!"

The portal closed and all were horrified beyond words.

THIRTY

AIN'T ABOUT THAT LIFE NO MORE

Cruising the Empyrean City streets in his brand-new car, Masai listened to his first completed track blasting on its stereo system. He wasn't feeling it. The commercialized shift in tempo and style bothered his authentic hip-hop sensibilities, from the throbbing beat, the crisp synthetic hook, to his topicless "get money, murder and bitches" flow.

Masai parked across the street from his penthouse building and stared at a billboard ad for his soon to be released track, "Hell Is Turnt Up On Them Streets" with Empyrean Killaz Music. Philly's chaotic devastation formed the backdrop as an iced-out Wrath Da Spitacular flossed with beautiful vixens and stacks of money.

"What would Mom and Dad think of me now," Masai thought as he took a hard look at himself in the rear-view mirror. He then sparked a blunt roach and smoked it down to a millimeter, contemplating whether his want of fame and fortune was worth him shirking his consecrated destiny. Through the rear-view mirror, Masai caught sight of Glacia, Hoodrat, and Johnny Fatal heading his way, visibly contused. He stepped out of his car and looked at them quizzically.

"Hardkore and 'Klysmo are dead, that's what!" Fatal bawled with contempt. "No thanks to you. Everybody knows you're Von Pyros' bitch!"

Masai squared off. Fatal was unyielding. Hoodrat and Glacia quickly ran interference.

"Gonna be a big shot rapper... What's the point in having all that power if you're not going to use 'em to help? Sell out."

Hoodrat pulled Fatal away as the condemnation pierced through Masai like hot daggers, flushing him with shame.

"Hey girl," Hoodrat said to Glacia, an afterthought. "I'm gonna calm Johnny. Relax his mind, you know?"

Glacia smirked, as if trying to follow Hoodrat's logic for her whoredom. Disgusted, she watched her escort Fatal away then turned to Masai. His eyes were downcast and for the first time since she'd known him, he appeared morose and fully helpless. It pained her to see him like that and she wished she had some type of esoteric power that could take his pain away, even if just for a little while. A sudden wave of inspiration hit as she finally got what Hoodrat was trying to relate to her. "Masai, can I use your shower?"

***

Water cascaded over Glacia's exquisite body as she showered, her heart pounding through her breasts. She was happy to have gained access into Masai's penthouse and was grateful another opportunity to be alone with him presented itself, but with his recent behaviors toward her, she had only the faintest notion of how to capitalize on the situation.

Glacia rounded into the living room looking innocently beautiful. Wearing one of Masai's tee shirts and a pair of his boxer shorts, her barefoot promenade was punctuated with a natural sway of the hips that would give rise to impotent men. But Masai hadn't noticed. He was on the balcony lick-rolling a blunt, stuck in the mire of his emotional funk.

Glacia stepped onto the balcony and gazed lovingly at him for a moment. She put her hand on the base of his neck and began massaging it gently. Masai gave her a look that dismissed her affection then poised to light the spliff.

In a spurt of fury, Glacia snatched the blunt from his mouth and tossed it over the balcony. Masai pounded his fist against the wall. Glacia walked off, defeated by his anger.

Masai squeezed his eyes tightly as the enormity of Fatal's judgement cut through him like a riptide. He tried reliving the exaltations and expectations of his parents and Kindred brethren, only to keep returning to the treachery that created Fatal's cowardly perception of him.

Fragrances of jasmine and vanilla wafted into Masai's nostrils as he suddenly became aware of soothing music playing softly behind him. He stepped back inside, annoyed yet intrigued.

Scented candles flickered as the stereo's silky rhythms turned the penthouse into a pavilion of relaxation and amour. Glacia was reclining on the sofa sipping a glass of wine, looking fine as all hell still adorned in his drawls. Masai wanted to stay angry but couldn't. Her moxie impressed him.

Glacia motioned Masai to her feet. Recognizing the ritual, he planted himself on the floor between her legs and she began palm-rolling his locs with hair pomade. Gradually the sensation of Glacia's touch became baptismal as he nestled in and closed his eyes, letting the moment purify him. She yanked his hair back abruptly, breaking the spell.

"I don't deserve the way you've been treating me lately," Glacia said, an unexpected seriousness in her voice. "I've never been anything but sweet to you and you didn't have to stop speaking to me. And if I did something wrong, why wouldn't you tell me?"

Masai looked up at her blankly. Glacia spun his head back around and resumed twisting his locs, filling in the beat of time in which he had not responded.

"It's just...we used to trust each other before," Glacia said, softening. "This may sound corny, but for a while I thought there was a unique, spiritual bond between us, like we were called to be together."

That just wrecked Masai. He gave her a look with a hand clutched over his heart that indicated he felt the same way.

"Then what you can do is trust me," Glacia said, her eyes imploring. "Share your pain with me."

191

Masai pushed himself to his feet, went onto the balcony and sagged against a wall. At that moment, he resented her for making him search himself for an explanation. Although he wanted to satisfy her with an answer, he thought that by expressing his deepest, unvoiced aches, it would make him feel smaller, more pathetic than ever. How do you explain that you are a deity sent here to save the world, but you're crippled by emotional issues, without sounding crazier than a crackhead?

Glacia followed him onto the balcony. Masai huddled to the floor, looked at her a moment, cleared his throat, then…

"I was sensitive to the energy currents within me since I was a young buck. It was a blessing to my family. It's a curse to me." Masai grew quiet again, overcome with emotion.

"Keep talking," Glacia said. "I love hearing your voice."

Masai exhaled a grievous breath. "Secretly I blamed my parents, for believing that I was something, that I'm not. Truth is, I was afraid."

"Afraid of what?" Glacia inquired.

"The pressure," Masai said, "Of letting them, everybody down. I was supposed to take care of my mother, protect her. And I didn't."

"You were just a kid then --"

"And I-I…I killed my dad," Masai blubbered, "With the power of my words…"

Masai turned away, embarrassed by his tears. Glacia touched his shoulder tentatively, gently. Fighting off his emotions, Masai roughly wiped his face dry and stood, collecting himself.

"So I vowed not to say shit after that. I wanted to teach myself to forget, to shut out that part of my life."

"I'm in that part of your life," Glacia said, turning to leave. Masai grabbed her hand, spinning her back to him.

"If I hurt you, too," Masai said, "I couldn't live, couldn't deal with that, yahmsayin'?"

"Life and death are both in the power of the tongue," Glacia said. "You have to teach yourself to ease the burden of your mind. Because right now we need you. I need you."

Glacia gave Masai a soft, almost deferential kiss. She then braced for an expectant brush off. But this time, Masai sought out her lips and kissed her tenderly at first, then fervently. He slid his hand around her waist and pulled her close against him. Then, under his power, the couple took flight and pirouetted into the sky.

Sparkling lights from Empyrean City below gave Glacia the sensation of vertigo. She quickly concealed the awe she felt by meeting his lips again. Vital fluids aroused their libidos like a soft fire as they undressed in mid-air, their clothes descending below...

***

Outside of the sick bay window, Emosha worried her discolored jaw as she looked in at Mister Mystiqal. He was lying motionless in a hospital bed, his body plugged with an array of tubes and IV's. Clumps of his hair was gone, and he looked like he had lost fifteen to twenty pounds. Earth Angel was on the edge of the bed praying over him in hushed tones.

"How's Mystiqal doing?" Kinetis asked as he approached Emosha at the glass.

"Mild radiation sickness," Emosha said. "He's resting now, but he'll be okay. Fortunately, he projected a mystic shield in time to buffer Faust's atomic blast. His cell count is metabolizing, and he should be waking soon."

Emosha and Kinetis walked into the infirmary, their entry snapping Earth Angel out of his prayer.

"Did you guys ever feel anything as unnaturally evil as that presence in the jungle?" Earth Angel asked, his voice timid yet anxious. "C'mon, I know it wasn't just me."

Dismissive, Kinetis projected a holograph of the Embryxx Industries' data from his metallic arm as he spoke.

"So let me get this straight. Dr. Tucci spawned some ancient End-Time demon clone for Aries, the same KLA double-agent that is now involved in a corporate fraud scheme that is bent on taking over the earth's precious metals, right?"

"We don't know if Aries acted alone, but that follows."

"We can also assume that Tucci got cold feet and snitched to the Hands of Wrath, who placed markings above the door to keep out demons, which meant Tucci hoped, believed that they and their deity could save him from those entities."

"Since the creatures couldn't get in Embryxx," Emosha said, "We were secured to bring in the assassins to kill Tucci."

"And I'm pretty sure those things outside were there to finish us off after Shadowstar, Skizzo and that Judas Guerrilla finished the job. Any accounts of hostile lifeforms like the —"

194

"—Didn't you feel it?!" Earth Angel screamed, his frustration level peaked. "Not because of my communion to the earth. It was…something deeper."

"I felt it, too," Emosha confessed.

"My ancestors often spoke of evil spirits from other dimensions that exist all around us," Kinetis said.

With a surprising boldness, Earth Angel shook Mystiqal up from his involuntary nap.

"Those monsters at Embryxx. Where'd they come from?"

"A predestined path —"

"No more bullshit."

Mystiqal sat up and blinked out the cobwebs. He reached his hand through empty space and pulled it back. A runty creature was in his grasp, wiggling and squealing frenetically.

"The fourth dimension," Mystiqal said, "Where other entities vibrate on a frequency right outside of your physical senses. There are many worlds that dwell outside of your earthly perceptions."

"How does any of this figure in with us?" Emosha questioned. "What did we do?"

"It's not what you did," Mystiqal said, releasing the shrieking creature back into empty space. "It's who you are. Descendants of original Kindreds. You are all members of the End-Time resistance force, the **CHILDREN OF THE APOCALYPSE**." Everyone traded stunned glances.

"But what about the disappearances?" Emosha asked.

Earth Angel jumped in. "Prophecy foretold that the souls of Kindred believers would be whisked out of this world and into the heavens in the End of Days."

"It's only a couple of us," Emosha said. "We might be in way over our head."

"Masai is the key," Kinetis said, his understanding resolute. "He has the greatest capacity to upset the evil cradle of power in this world."

Earth Angel turned to Mystiqal darkly, his tone accusing. "You've known all about this and you've never said anything."

"It would not be destiny if I interposed my supernatural knowledge," Mystiqal said.

"Tell that to Kid Hardkore and Kataklysmo."

THIRTY-ONE

Tilted Off Her Axiss

In the financial district of Empyrean City, Supreme Maffmattixx stood at the edge of a building rooftop reading the illuminated news as it spiraled an adjacent skyscraper:

"A deadly explosion of a Central American laboratory compound in which sixteen of the world's leading geneticists and seven mutant-terrorists, including Hands of Wrath leader Johann Faust, were killed was clearly a mutant-terrorist attack, newly appointed global ambassador Dorian Von Pyros said this afternoon. He blamed the attack on Faust and his extremists, and the bombing was revenge for the execution of the KLA's leader Osiris Jackson..."

Maffmattixx turned his attention to the rear of the Empyrean Ventures' warehouse. Several workers were carefully unloading huge portable tanks and crates from a truck onto a forklift. As the loaded forklift went into the building, Maffmattixx teleported --

-- He then came into physical being inside of the warehouse and quickly took cover behind a large container. As the loaded forklift passed by, Maffmattixx inconspicuously scooted behind it to the far end of the room. He ducked behind a stack of crates and watched as the forklift driver pulled up to a pressurized elevator door, eye-dentiscanned and went inside.

As the elevator ascended, Maffmattixx deadpanned a look around, making sure all was clear. His eyes then zeroed in on the commercial invoice label affixed to a crate in front of him:

"Exported from Motumbo Incorporated, South Africa - Imported to Empyrean Ventures, North America."

Maffmattixx quietly unhinged the top of the crate and raised it, revealing heaps of gold coins. He fingered the krugerrand, confounded. He then moved to another crate, divulging its contents. It was stockpiled with iridium metals.

The sound of footsteps approaching. Maffmattixx crouched behind the crates. A security guard's looming shadow appeared in his field of vision with a pistol extended in both hands, cop-style...

A quick scuffle behind the crates. The Guard emerged, moved to the elevator, eye-dentiscanned and went inside.

The Guard exited the elevator on the top floor and stood just inside a vast transport control room. The place was utilitarian and sterile, a reflection of its apathetic atmosphere. Technicians were everywhere, running through their protocol.

The Guard began to walk through, examining the surroundings in more detail. There was a lattice of pipes and conduits above, galactical maps and satellite images on computer screens. At the far end of the room was the complex superstructure, the TPZ One Thousand, its numerous coaxial cables and connecters leading to a colossal screen which displayed the twinkling infiniteness of space. Workers were unloading crates onto a large platform in front of it.

Facing the huge screen was a hair-weaved technician wearing unique-fingered gloves and a headset. She passed her hands over the screen and "conducted" a grid to overlay the cosmos. The screen responded to wherever she motioned as a set of coordinates zeroed in on a planet in a distant galaxy.

Just then, Aries entered with a tour of dignitaries.

"And this is our transport control room," Aries said. "As you can see on the Cosmo-Vision screen, our shipments are preparing to be teleported."

"What is this thing you call teleported?" A dignitary asked. The Cosmo-Vision conductor turned around to address the dignitary. It was Axiss.

"The process of making information vanish from one place and reappear in another," Axiss said. She then gestured, and the shipment of crates disappeared from the platform, whisked through the Cosmo-Vision screen and astonishingly landed on a faraway planet. "They'll be transmitted faster than the speed of light to their given destination."

"And much more securely without giving away their initial location," Aries added. "It's all based on quantum physics. Come, I have more to show you." Aries then escorted them out of the room.

"Intergalactic trade," the Guard stated resolutely as he shapeshifted into Supreme Maffmattixx on the move. "Was it worth it, selling humanity out?"

"Look, I'm a businesswoman," Axiss said. "Do you have any idea what our riches are worth off-world? The Brotherhood of the Vampyrians have been bartering our precious metals for alien technology a very long time. Since we can't beat 'em, I figured I might as well join them and get paid in the process."

"When knowledge is born, the universe will align itself with Masai's power," Maffmattixx said

"Whatever," Axiss said as she signaled the dozen or so techs and workers to move in, morphing into grinning Vampyrians. "Your death moments from now is inevitable."

"It won't be a homicide, bitch," Maffmattixx snarled as he struck a battle stance. "It'll be revolutionary suicide!"

Axiss' body transformed a percolating solar black and she flung her solar axe at Maffmattixx. He did a gravity-defying flip, evading -- the axe obliterated a chair behind him and returned to her hand. Maffmattixx landed between a handful of demons in the form of Sheer Will the Elder. In a matter of seconds, they were taken apart by his powerful weakness-detecting blows...

***

Meanwhile in the penthouse, Glacia guided Masai back on the bed as they kissed feverishly, their nude bodies glistening from love's heat. A deep, whispery moan escaped her mouth as his lips moved across her neck to her breasts. Glacia rested her hands on his chest as she rode him sensually...

Axiss moved in and attacked. Sheer Will morphed into a blade-wielding Osiris and they exchanged powerful blocks and strikes, with Osiris getting the upper hand. Axiss snuck in and delivered a devastating blow that went through Osiris' telekinetic shield, sending him flying across the room. Dazed, he reverted to Maffmattixx as she closed in...

Masai rolled Glacia over. He angled her thighs back with his upper body weight, forcing her feet to arch for the ceiling. Glacia clutched the sheets as a pleasurable shudder moved through her like a cyclone. Masai interlaced his hand with hers as the lovemaking became increasingly more spirited with each thrust, building...

Axiss whacked Maffmattixx in the stomach then slugged him in the face. Stunned, Maffmattixx opened a portal in front of the doors and scrambled toward it. Axiss hurled her axe, cleaving him between the shoulder blades. Maffmattixx slumped lifeless and the portal closed just ahead of him...

With an explosive climax, the lover's hands opened like a flower in full bloom.

THIRTY-TWO

HELL OF A PARTY

Masai was fast asleep with a rare look of peace and contentment on his face. A lulled Glacia snuggled cozily under his arm, idly tracing his pectoral birthmark with her finger as she listened to his heartbeat. She looked as if she wanted that moment to last forever.

Glacia's eyes drifted over to Masai's architectural designs that adorned the walls. It touched her to know that he hadn't totally abandoned his concepts for an environment-friendly city system. She then caught sight of a picture frame with a crinkled letter inside. Curious, she clutched a sheet and got out of bed to get a closer look. It was the balled-up girlfriend/boyfriend note from Mr. Watson's class. She formed a cherished smile.

Browsing the wall further, she inadvertently knocked the Epistles of True Wisdom off the nightstand. Photos from inside the sacred book sprawled about. Glacia gathered the pictures and stole glances at them, becoming enthralled by a specific one. It was of her adorably pudgy self, Masai and Ashanti on the Uptown's rooftop many moons ago. She examined the photo cursorily, trying to see everything in the image; from her favorite barrettes in her hair, to the gritty North Philly skyline, to Supreme Maffmattixx standing in the background...

"Maffmattixx wasn't...couldn't have been there, could he?" She then began leafing through the rest of the pictures. Maffmattixx was prominent in several of them.

Glacia placed the photos back and closed the book, her eyes riveting on the embossed symbol of the winged sun disk on its cover. She whirled to the birthmark on Masai's chest. Then to the book again. Then back to Masai. She wanted to wake him and ask about his relationship to it but was afraid that it might create distance between them again. Confused and overwhelmed, Glacia hurriedly retrieved her clothing.

Moments later, a fully dressed Glacia stood over Masai as he slept, the Epistles of True Wisdom in her grasp. She kissed his cheek, stared a moment longer then left.

***

With the Kindred's sacred book in her hand, Glacia gave a push to a door which was slightly ajar.

"Supreme Maffmattixx?" Glacia called as she stepped inside the dimly lit room, panning around as she moved through. "I know you were at the Uptown building with us... And I'm betting you're here to prevent the eagle from thinking he's a chicken."

"Glacia…" A voice whispered from within the room.

"Maffmattixx, is that you?" Glacia said, her gaze stopping at a silhouetted man seated with his legs crossed and his shirt open within the shadows.

"Nay, my beautiful Ice Empress." The man rose and slowly moved to her, emerging into the light. It was the unmistakable figure of Von Pyros. Glacia dropped the book and struck a battle pose. "Where's Maffmattixx?"

Von Pyros removed his shirt. All three of his eyes were penetrating. "By my side, all realms of existence will pay homage to your exquisite beauty as we share ecstasy that defies all description."

Glacia's fury waned under his arcane charm. "Where…" Beguiled, she clutched her hair to one side, offering her neck. Von Pyros leaned in, bearing his now elongated canines and began to feed on her sensually.

***

In the Empyrean Hotel, a huge reception was taking place with all the pomp and circumstance intergalactic trade and currency could buy. Many of Empyrean City's social elite were in attendance, enjoying the music, dancing, food and champagne.

Axiss, bedecked in unique striking jewelry and a tight sheath of a dress, hobnobbed coquettishly amongst the suits and power ties.

Von Pyros entered and sat at the Table of Honor, flanked by former President Reynolds and Lilith. Beaming with glee, Von Pyros swiveled to the stampeding mob rushing to the dance floor as a popular line dance tune came on.

"I don't think this was a good idea," Lilith whispered, dampening the mood.

"What is wrong with throwing a party?" Von Pyros asked. "Especially when in a few hours, the humans will be handing over the keys to the earth to us."

"It's my duty to advise you against such trivial acts," Lilith said. "Besides, they haven't given it to us. Yet."

"What do you propose that I do?"

"Kill Masai now," Lilith said. "Send everything at him before he awakens from his induced slumber."

"Lilith, relax," Von Pyros said as he stood. "Have a drink."

"Dorian, please…" Von Pyros headed for the dance floor, falling in rhythmic step with Axiss and the rest of the line dancers. Lilith sat alone at the table, perturbed.

***

Masai's eyes fluttered open as he slowly focused on reality. He touched the side of the bed. No Glacia. He sat up. Looked at the nightstand. No Epistles of True Wisdom. Shit.

Masai closed his eyes, allowing his consciousness to travel at lightspeed through the psyches of the inhabitants of Empyrean City, trying to locate Glacia.

His brow suddenly furrowed as he passed over a familiar consciousness that was safeguarded by a psychic defense. Masai zeroed in on it like a sniper with his target in the crosshairs. He penetrated their inferior mental fortress and uncovered a mind filled with self-ambition and treachery.

Masai opened his eyes like he'd been snapped out of a deep medicated sleep, a surprised but determined look on his face.

Moments later, garbed in one of his tailor-made outfits, Masai looked around his penthouse a moment, seemingly taking it all in for the last time. He then turned and exited.

THIRTY-THREE

VENGEANCE IS MINE, Y⊙

Masai pushed through the door of the Empyrean Ventures' warehouse and was immediately met by a guard trying to halt his migration. Without breaking stride, he dispatched the guard easily with a two-piece and headed for the stairwell.

Masai raced up the stairs under the grip of his telepathic compulsion. He emerged on the top floor and cut across a pool of unoccupied cubicles and terminals with roving financial news. He then moved through an empty receptionist area and heard the faint sound of a man's voice echoing from behind a half-open door labeled, "Transport Control Room." Moving closer revealed the man carrying on multiple conversations, stockbroker-style.

"If the Venusians want that much palladium, they better not offer anything as primitive as three-dimensional printers. Play hard like an ol' folks toenail and get back to me... Brad, there had better be a good reason why the Andromedans are buying bullion from the Saturnians and not from us…"

Masai girded himself for his psychical-driven encounter as he slid into the room, quietly closing the door behind him. At the Cosmo-Vision screen was a black man wearing a custom European suit. Anxiety trickled like cold water in the chambers of his body as the man half-turned --

It was ARIES. The dude was Aries. Aries.

"Those Vegan analysts don't know their ass from a hole in the wall…" The hairs on the back of Aries' neck prickled. He pivoted and saw Masai moving toward him like a panther stalking its prey.

"Always knew one day you would come to avenge your mother," Aries said, removing his jacket and tie. "I've been wanting to kick your ass a long time." He flung his earphone away and squared off with Masai for an ol' school fair one…

***

At the Table of Honor, Lilith sat before her carefully arranged spread of tarot cards. She took a nervous breath…

Masai's face warped with rage as he led off, exchanging remarkably fast blocks and counters. Aries took advantage of an opening and threw a thunderous haymaker that grazed Masai, staggering him back. Aries sneered.

Aries plodded in throwing powerful blows. Masai parried and caught him with a barrage of speedy wallops that flattened Aries on a desk, decimating it. Masai coolly did a Cee-Walk dance. Aries got up, brandished a pair of nunchucks and expertly twirled them. Masai half-circled...

Lilith plucked a card: "The Ace of Celestial Vengeance." Her eyes widened in horror...

Aries furiously drove Masai back, his weapon interchanging at will. Masai evaded, ducking just under the mighty swing of the nunchucks that exploded through the sheet rock behind him like confetti. He then countered the thwack of a mace and delivered a powerful combination, finishing with a kick that slammed Aries back against the Cosmo-Vision screen...

Lilith, Guerrilla and two dozen armed men raced down the street to the warehouse...

Masai pressed his attack. He gave a feint then unleashed an unrelenting barrage of hooks, crosses and elbow strikes...

Lilith and the troops charged up the warehouse steps...

Aries snuck in a ferocious blow that shook Masai's equilibrium like he just got crossed over. Masai quickly got back on defense. He eluded the whoosh of a hammer that blasted through a crate of gold coins. Aries then looped a whip around Masai's legs, yanking him to the floor. He made a slit-throat gesture, closing in --

Masai looked sharply at a crate. It darted over and crashed Aries in the chest, sending him flying across the room.

Aries staggered to his feet and lumbered in, the whip whirling savagely. He coiled it around Masai's throat, threw the whip's handle over the piping above, then dove for the handle, yanking hard. Masai was jerked upward by the neck, his feet pinwheeling off the ground. Aries' face knotted tight as he pulled with all his strength. Masai clawed at the whip desperately, his life flashing…

Masai gritted through the pain and asphyxiation and generated a telekinetic dragon-hand. It exhaled a blast of fire that severed the whip. Masai dropped to the ground gasping as Aries tumbled backwards, slamming hard to the floor.

"You can't win," Aries said as he stirred up, his red armor covering and a spear in his clutches. "See, this isn't about faith, it is about power, something Osiris and Ashanti knew nothing about. They were fools, fools risking their whole world for a fruitless cause and an impotent deity…"

Masai's breathing slowed and leveled as Aries' words twisted in his heart. Cosmic energy particles began to dazzle around his cocked fist as everything he had been through came barreling at him in an instant, the darkness that eclipsed his parent's lives, the remorse, the self-pity, revenge… A powder keg of rage just beneath the threshold of his conscious mind flared to its zenith on the end of his wrist.

"But absolute power will be mine, once I kill you," Aries snarled as he leveled his spear for attack. "Throughout the galaxies, I'll be known as… Aries the Godkiller!!"

Aries lunged forward wildly, thrusting his spear. Masai parried and swung, landing the death blow --

Aries' eyes bugged out in an agonizing gaze as dashes of cosmic energy branched off into a spidery network across the surface of his armored body --

Inside the mind of Aries, the cosmic energy throbbed and beelined its way across synapses in the brain, causing an audible cracking breach, splitting his psyche --

Aries' body disintegrated as his mind and spiritual essence frittered away into nothingness. Masai posed in the striking position a la Bruce Lee style, his expression a strange mix of shock, relief and cold satisfaction.

Suddenly the door smashed open. Guerrilla and the troops were clogging the doorway, aiming.

"Try some shit now," Guerrilla said.

Masai's nostrils flared as he reacted --

"Wait!" Lilith yelled. "The Master wants to see you."

THIRTY-FOUR

INNERSTANDING

With his hood obscuring his face, Masai strolled into Von Pyros' inner sanctum accompanied by Lilith, Guerrilla and the armed-at-the ready entourage. He wasn't threatening, but they weren't taking any chances.

Masai and his escorts came to a halt in front of Von Pyros who was reclining on his baroque throne, cooler than a fan. Von Pyros flashed a signal with his eyes to Lilith. She about-faced and headed out. Masai took off his hood and glared hard at his former social worker, then at the enemy who he overstood had total command of his life from the jump.

"So you've been watching me with your all-seeing eye, playin' me," Masai said, "Vampyro."

"I was beginning to believe you really didn't know who I was," Von Pyros said as his appearance began to morph into a form that was a far cry from the aristocrat from before. He was now **VAMPYRO, THE SON OF PERDITION**, his skin a corpse bluish white. His trendy gothic attire exposed the subsisting eye on his chest and his hair crackled with wild spectral fire. "A brilliant strategy, since I cannot read minds."

"All warfare is based on deception," Masai said.

"True indeed."

Vampyro arose from his throne and wandered over to a door suspended in space. He motioned Masai over courteously. Masai didn't budge.

"I understand your reservations," Vampyro said. "If you please..." Masai treaded over cautiously.

"Your father was also fearful of the intoxicating aroma of power. But as I informed him, doors can be opened that were otherwise shut, all lifeforms will bend to your will and influence and all possessions in this world and others can be yours," Vampyro opened the door, "And everything in them."

Masai entered the dimensional gateway and stopped in his tracks. Dim. Intoxicating. Sinful. Torches burned in sconces on the otherworldly-glyphed wall. Teasing glimpses of female debauchery decorated the immense chamber amid flowing taffeta. Masai was hesitant yet intrigued.

Before Masai could think, two temptresses flanked him. Their sinfully wonderful eyes and figures conspired to make him weak as they floated their delicate hands over his body.

Glacia then stepped out of the shadows, her gown provocative and her face now burning with the sexiness of an enchantress. She swished over to Masai enticingly.

"I know you're powerful, Boo, in more ways than one," Glacia said as she lingered in, her voice a beguiling opiate. "But you're tired, tired of hurting, of feeling torn inside..."

Masai's mind spun in a hazy distortion of time and space. Vampyro flushed with delight as he watched Masai succumb to their bewitching rhapsody.

"We're establishing a new kingdom," Glacia said. "Your pain will be just a memory. Join us. Be my sovereign..."

Glacia kissed Masai torridly. Her lips were euphoric as ecstasy surged through him in ways he never thought possible. Every secret feeling, lustful thought and sexual inclination was expressed in that kiss. But the eroticism didn't touch their experiences, adoration and friendship at all, upon which their connection was inextricably bound. That understanding exposed to him what Glacia truly was at that moment, an evil succubus whose power was only in his acquiescence. Fighting with every ounce of his will, Masai pried away, an anti-climax to a lustful spell.

"Loose from her," Masai commanded. Transcendental energy traveled from his mouth to Glacia's spirit, catapulting her head back. Scores of evil spirits escaped from her body and wasted away into the atmosphere. The temptresses fearfully backed away.

Masai signaled Glacia toward the gateway exit. As she stepped past in compliance, he gave her a proprietary smack on the butt. Clutched his crotch. What.

Vampyro's hair crackled a little higher and wilder, Masai's cocksure swag having its effect.

"So whatchu want," Masai asked sarcastically, "Riches? To be the king of the world? The universe?"

"Is the ace not higher than the king?" Vampyro said. "No, Masai. True power rests behind the throne."

"You're just a mega-maniacal nutball havin' a beef with the Creator," Masai said. "Or did you forget?"

"I know the Creator of all creations exists, better than anyone," Vampyro said as he looked skyward grandly. "The formation of this world was an indescribable spectacle! Infinitely more majestic than the birth of ones' own child..." Vampyro closed his eyes and prattled on, trance-like. "I can still envision my master's rage as dominion of this world was not handed to him... the most beautiful and gifted angel... should have been ruler... over eons, fury that defies all description..." He then opened his eyes, completely calm. "Mankind has perpetuated humanity into believing in evolution, not creation. I shall relish in tormenting their souls eternally, for if they reject the existence of the Most High, they reject me also."

"Mankind perpetuated humanity...?" Masai queried.

"Surely you know of earth's gene-pool problem," Vampyro said. "Mankind...kind of like a man, as opposed to human?"

Masai zoned out a split second as his mind flashbacked:

In the execution chamber: Lilith and the glass-visored demoniacal faces of the agents...

Maffmattixx at the penthouse door: "Cats like Guerrilla... Every brother ain't a brother, 'nahmean?"

Von Pyros' parlor: "Mutant-terrorists are such monsters," Von Pyros said, "Makes you wonder what's inside of people..."

"There are others, who accept their gifts and use them for the benefit of *Mankind*..."

"Tsk, tsk," Vampyro said as he held up a copy of the Epistles of True Wisdom, bringing Masai back to awareness. "I shall digress to compensate for your amnesia."

Vampyro quickly leafed through the sacred book and found his text:

"'And Wrath the Conqueror smited the devils and cast them back to their wicked domains; that the few will seek refuge in the HIGH TEMPLES OF THE EXALTED PEOPLE, spreading their wickedness amongst their inner dwellings --'"

"-- Until Wrath the Conqueror's return in the End of Days," Masai said, finishing the scriptural quote. "So a couple of y'all devils hid inside the bodies of ruling class humans while you built your shit back up, preparing for a rematch. But why procreate with humans? Why not fuck your own ugly bitches and spawn your own monster bastards?"

Vampyro smirked, tossing the book aside. "Within the secret confines of elite mortals, my minions could further our domination agenda, but be less advanced than us so we could not justify treating them morally. Besides, humans are considered the most primitive and vile creatures throughout the galaxies, capable of unleashing immense destruction upon each other. Hiding within them was a logical progression."

Vampyro paced away and portals began to open beneath his feet with each step. Inside the portals, an ambiguous image began to materialize fully...

A group of young punks were shooting craps on an inner-city street corner. A small Vampyrian was perched on the shoulder of one of the punks, invisible to all.

"Over millenium, legions of souls are recruited, humans and hybrids alike, every minute, every second..."

The Vampyrian slapped the punk, prompting him to whip out a gun and fire at the dice holder. Everyone scattered.

"...Eating and excreting their way through their pathetic existences, most unaware of the supernatural war that they are participants in..."

A priest stood in a schoolyard observing catholic schoolchildren at play. A Vampyrian materialized and slapped the priest, jostling him. Impelled by a sudden twisted lust, the priest snatched up a little boy and took off, with school staff giving chase. The priest forced the boy into a car, jumped in and peeled off...

"...Millions of souls filled with murder, madness and mayhem coursing through their bloodstreams, battle-ready for the confrontation of the multiverses..."

The priest leaned in, unzipping his fly... Von Pyros stopped walking and the portals closed.

"This is just the beginning of many galaxy takeovers. Just imagine, you as Master General of my enigmatic armies."

"Sounds like a mega-maniacal nutball to me."

Vampyro's hair flared wildly as he projected a malicious force blast that crashed Masai through a wall, crumbling it. In fact, the whole chamber began to deteriorate, revealing --

A hellish realm that spanned a thousand times its original size. Flaming pits existed everywhere, filled with screaming souls enslaved in eternal torment and sorrow.

Masai struggled to rise as he covered his nose from the foul smell of the netherworld. Suddenly he was yanked to his feet by Vampyro and slung hard against the rocks. Masai blearily lurched forward to launch an attack -- Vampyro slammed a roundhouse under his cheek. He then stepped back as a handful of Vampyrians began assailing Masai, one ferocious blow after another. Devilish bystanders were going ape-shit wild as they gave Masai the beating of his life, with Guerrilla sneaking in a few cheap shots.

Vampyro force-blasted him again. Masai flew about fifty yards across a flaming chasm and collapsed in a heap. His face was glazed with sweat and blood and his mind was clouded with resignation.

Suddenly, a beam of light radiated out of the damnable sky and shined down like the hand of God. Masai labored to lift his head as spiritual pleas that only he could perceive began to cry out, the voices an affecting cacophony of distorted echoes...

Masai listened as everything he had been told was being channeled by the voices; the stories of Kindred love and survival, the persistent admonitions that he was a spiritual being having a human existence, the legend, the prophecy, a host of considerable burdens that were thrusted upon him without his consent. But now there was a difference. He now understood, overstood and innerstood that the divine utterances weren't coming from anywhere but from a long, forgotten place, the realm inside of himself, where the highest version of the grandest vision he had of himself resided.

Converting the lofty appeals into inner power, Masai staggered to his feet as he began to settle into the truth of his very being...

THIRTY-FIVE

EYE FOR AN ALL-SEEING EYE

Glacia and the rest of the Children of the Apocalypse appeared at the hanging doorway just as scores of manic Vampyrians moved across the hellscape like a swarm of insects, converging on Masai.

Johnny Fatal brandished his Glocks. "Let's go!"

Emosha held him back. "Wait!"

Everyone looked on in awe and wonder --

Masai, now **WRATH THE CONQUEROR,** stood with a mighty authority. His left eye blazed and his body was sequined with stars. Cosmic winds blew his wardrobe and locs and in his face was a savage kind of intensity not seen before.

The armed guards, now Vampyrians, poised to fire. Wrath panned over them nightmarishly. Their weapons exploded dramatically out of their grasps in a series of staggered bursts.

Guerrilla frightfully backed away as hordes of Vampyrians began to circle Wrath apprehensively, growling and hissing.

Wrath jab stepped. They jerked back with fear and respect. Then, under Vampyro's command – all hell broke loose.

Wrath's power was unlike anything seen before. His deadly hands of kung fu changed intermittently into the animals of the Shaolin system, his limbs of fury mirroring their corresponding styles and attributes. With psychic speed, foresight and an inhuman level of skill, Wrath dodged fiendish attacks from behind without even looking and every block was a putrefied strike. Heinous specters billowed into the atmosphere with each blow he delivered. With his rage directed and power fine-tuned, Wrath had entered that internal place where life and death had formed a solemn pact, where two seemingly opposing forces progressed toward the shared goal of survival, by any means necessary.

Inundated by a seemingly endless flood of Vampyrians, Wrath took to the air on telekinetic winds.

"Split." With that said, Wrath's body strikingly exploded and splintered off into legions of doppelgangers. Vampyrians were taken apart by their esoteric one-hitter quitters, leaving a wave of ash and withering phantasms in their wake.

When the last Vampyrian was dispatched, the multitude of doppelgangers reformed back into the mighty Wrath the Conqueror as he touched down onto a jutting hunk of rock several yards from Vampyro.

At the suspended doorway, the Children of the Apocalypse were stunned. They couldn't believe what they had just seen, what they were privy to bear witness to. They now brimmed with heightened anticipation as if it was just before a heavyweight title fight, the adversarial intensity between Wrath the Conqueror and Vampyro eye to eye.

"It seems the chains that had enslaved your mind are broken," Vampyro said.

"Manifesting the highest levels of consciousness is child's play to me," Wrath said.

"This is my final decree," Vampyro scowled. "Herald my legions into the future or perish."

"Fuck no."

"Very well."

Vampyro chopped the ground, breaking about a third of the bedrock off. Wrath took to the otherworldly skies as the ground beneath his feet fell into a flaming abyss.

Vampyro force-blasted – Wrath telekinetically drew up rubble from the terrain. It encased his body just as the blast made contact, knocking him a half-mile back in the air.

Wrath exploded out of the rock formation grandly. Then from that distance, he expertly threw punches in the air, "shadowboxing". Vampyro reeled as a blitzkrieg of telekinetic blows connected to his body and face.

Vampyro shook the blows off, his eyes disbelieving. His chest-eye suddenly crackled with occult energy and fired --

"Stop." Prompted by Wrath's authority, the occult blast stopped stone-still inches from him --

"Switch." Wrath and Vampyro both disappeared then reappeared in each other's place --

222

"**Accelerate.**" The occult blast sped up again and with the same velocity, walloped Vampyro and engulfed him with a concussive arctic fire. Vampyro let out a bloodcurdling roar as he spiraled through the air and crashed into the inside face of a cliff. A tide of evil spirits spewed out of him and wasted away as the corrosive blast freezer-burned his physical form to bone, to embers, to naught.

Wrath touched down just as the hellish realm transformed back into the throne room. He became the power center as the Children of the Apocalypse rushed over with a new respect, all on his top. Glacia beamed with genuine attraction mixed with a newly intense awe. After all, she was in love with a God. But Wrath's face betrayed all nuances of their accolades.

"It ain't over," Wrath said.

"Didn't you just destroy him?" Glacia asked.

"The End-Time leader long-prophesied ain't gonna be defeated so easily," Wrath replied.

"What's his agenda?" Kinetis asked.

"To conquer the multiverses through diplomacy," Mister Mystiqal said as he meandered over, thumbing through the copy of the Epistles of True Wisdom. "One galaxy at a time."

"Can't do that if he's dead," Fatal said.

"Vampyro is supposed to be without a soul," Earth Angel said as he snatched the book from Mister Mystiqal and handed it to Wrath.

"Whatever that means," Fatal said.

"Demonic possession?" Hoodrat asked.

"Even a demon-possessed person has a soul," Emosha said.

"An infernal being having an earthly existence would have to have a scientific answer to a supernatural question," Wrath said as he leafed through the book. Having found his text, "Peep this: 'And in that time, there will be two Sons of Perdition, one born of providence, the other by men of the authority; that the latter shall be wrought with more power than the first and that no spirit shall dwell within it.' See what I'm sayin'?"

Everyone looked at him, confounded.

"A clone," Wrath said. "It's soulless, you feel me? This bridges the gap between the physical and spiritual realms."

"The clone is probably in effect somewhere right now carrying out the plan," Fatal said.

"Omigod," Glacia gasped in sudden revelation. "The Global Peace Covenant!"

THIRTY-SIX

RETURN OF THE CONQUEROR

Outside of Philadelphia's gloriously ornate City Hall, a gargantuan video screen existed above the make-shift stage as thousands prepared to watch the signing of the Global Peace Covenant with great expectancy. Police barricades, SWAT trucks and media from around the world adorned the evening streets as dozens of VIP's took up residence on the stage.

The CLONE OF VON PYROS rose from among the dignitaries and took the podium amid ass-kissy applause.

"My fellow citizens of the earth," Von Pyros said with a bogus warmth as he settled the crowd down, "Ladies and gentlemen of the press and great luminaries from around the world. Here, in the City of Brotherly Love, the greatest event in the history of the world is about to take place: The signing of the Global Peace Covenant!"

The crowd thundered their approval as they continued to do from everything that he said.

"Speaking on behalf of our distinguished world leaders and Kindred representatives, we contend that peace can only be achieved through global accord. So for the next seven years, all economic sanctions will be lifted! There will be one world religion! One world currency! Because we are one world! Together we can make this a great place for Mankind!"

Von Pyros' triumphant and charismatic speech erupted the crowd into ovation. One by one the dignitaries greeted him at center stage and then autographed the historic document. When the last dignitary had signed, they all hugged and waved to the flashing of a million bulbs.

Suddenly, a thin line of electric light rifted across the night sky. A loud collective gasp outpoured from the crowd as everyone looked skyward, mystified. A breach opened in the sky and Wrath the Conqueror egressed out of it, followed by Glacia, Earth Angel, Kinetis, Emosha, Hoodrat, Johnny Fatal and Mister Mystiqal: The Children of the Apocalypse. All eyes fixated on their grandiose descent as chants of his legendary name began to flow through the crowd:

"Wrath the Conqueror! Wrath the Conqueror!"

Von Pyros and the VIP's were quickly ushered into City Hall by security.

"This is an unbelievable spectacle!" Jordyn Martinez screamed as her cameraman stumble-ran backwards, filming the uncanny spectacle. "A capacity crowd is present, and they are witnessing what could possibly be one of the most inspirational moments in history! A religious phenomenon! There is pandemonium everywhere as what many on hand believe to be is Wrath the Conqueror and his archangels floating down from the heavens!"

The Children of the Apocalypse touched down about a block away from the stage beside the famous LOVE statue. Three-hundred and sixty degrees of guns were trained on them and a fussilade of red dots danced over their bodies.

"Ah-ight," Fatal said, "What now, yo?"

Wrath stepped forward. There was a majestic power in his thuggish gait as his image appeared on the giant screen.

"Drop your weapons," Wrath said, his voice commanding all. Law enforcement everywhere began laying their firearms on the ground and the red dots vanished from their anatomy. Wrath then gazed fiercely into the cameras. **"Now get the fuck outta here."**

Under his order, mobs of people began to haul ass aimlessly, running roughshod over everything and everybody. Wrath just shrugged in "my bad" fashion.

In the confusion, Guerrilla stepped out of Kinetis and phased into a frantic passerby. Disoriented, Kinetis wandered off unnoticed.

A SWAT agent's body suddenly plummeted from a building and splatted to the asphalt nearby. Wrath looked skyward, his "cosmic vision" allowing him to see through the building to its summit. In his celestial scope, Axiss was hacking through the sharpshooters in a murderous frenzy, the rooftop her killing field.

"That's that chick with the solar axes up there trashin' the cops," Wrath said.

Emosha reacted, drawing her sword. Glacia held her back.

"Let me deal with her." Glacia then angled through the scattering crowd toward the building.

As Emosha watched Glacia go inside, she felt a recognizable presence near the building's entrance, a different kind of vibration from the rest. Shadowstar's ambiguous form began to materialize, sword in hand. He waded through the crowd, egging her on.

"Emosha," Wrath called as he watched her stew with barely contained hatred, "Do your thing."

Like Christmas morning. Emosha passionately pounded Wrath on his chest then charged over to Shadowstar. And as if in an improvised dance, the light and dark combatants resumed their dynamic duel to the death.

Wrath looked catty-corner, his celestial eye tracking a concentrated phantasmic trail leading inside of City Hall.

"The rest of y'all," Wrath said, "With me."

With conviction and purpose, Wrath and his remaining party walked briskly toward City Hall.

Hoodrat slowed a few paces and scratched the air with a finger, creating a furrowed gateway. A Hoodrat brood rushed out of it, tatted up ungodly to the hilt.

"I'ma call you Fatalianika," Hoodrat said to her new offspring. "Let's catch up with your dad." Hoodrat and Fatalianika scurried up close to Johnny Fatal, who smirked at his sexually transmitted dependent with dismay.

Lilith was perched on top of the city's forty-five-foot Clothespin statue like Moses on Mount Sinai. Mumbling indistinct but understandably evil, she dramatically slapped a card down to the ground, the "Stirring of Hosts".

Suddenly, wicked shrieks charged the air with a dark tension. Human faces within the crowd began to contort with pain and rage, morphing, changing into demons. Fully transformed, they began to highball toward Wrath and the Children of the Apocalypse with reckless abandon.

"Matrix," Wrath declared, his words twisting time and space in a way his peers could not believe. Demons all around began to move in slow motion, their fabric of reality altered. It seemed to them that the Children of the Apocalypse were a mile away.

"The clone's in City Hall," Wrath said as he hurled a telekinetic cannonball at Lilith, slamming her hard against a building amid fluttering tarot cards. "Mister Mystiqal, Earth Angel. Crowd control. Levitate the people to safety with your controls of gravity."

Self-doubt washed over Earth Angel's face. "I only have earth control powers."

"The earth's not just plants and the four elements," Wrath said. "There's gravity, magnetic fields, electricity, you feel me? Breakin' it down further, since humans comprise the same elements as --"

Mystiqal interjected with a covetous tone. "I believe an aerial assault from the two of us would be most effective."

"We'll do as he says." With that, Earth Angel took to the sky, his spell of inferiority broken. Mystiqal hesitantly followed behind him.

"Johnny Fatal, Hoodrat. City Hall," Wrath said. "Secure the area. I'll be there in a minute."

"What are you gonna do?" Hoodrat asked as they backpedaled toward City Hall. Wrath gestured, and the demons gradually began to return to wildness. Wrath turned to Hoodrat and curled a snide grin, reminiscent of his father. "I just love a good rumble."

With a fiend-startling battle cry, Wrath dove into the demons as they barreled forward maniacally. He became a supernatural fighting circus, dismantling demonic flesh and dismissing orgies of apparitions with the greatest of ease.

A pack of demons took to the buildings behind Wrath, wall-crawling up high with bug-like dexterity. They leaped off, swooping down toward him --

"Pop." With that said, pouncing demons spontaneously combusted, exploding out of the sky like fireworks.

Wrath took to the air. Demonic eyes followed as he sailed over and landed by Philly's mammoth Clothespin statue.

"Grow." Wrath's body immediately increased in proportionate size to seventy-five feet. Demons ignorantly swarmed in as he ripped the Clothespin from its base...

***

Glacia emerged onto the rooftop in dreaded fascination. Sharpshooters were dead on the roof's floor. As she waded through the carnage, her eyes caught a glimpse of the

Clothespin statue ascending into the skyline then descending speedily from view. She looked over the roof's edge and saw a giant Wrath the Conqueror swinging homeruns at demons.

"Money, power, respect... That's what it's all about, right?" Glacia whirled to the sound of Axiss' voice. A slight breeze stirred Axiss' normally impeccable weave and she was wearing Maffmattixx's jacket that fit a bit oversized on her.

"That's your problem," Glacia said, secretly cupping a playing card delineated with razor-sharpened ice. "Always looking for happiness outside of yourself."

"I could never be like you, girl," Axiss said. "You had everything. I was just lucky I made it to my eleventh birthday before..." Axiss' voice trailed off as she wiped a lone tear away. "I know how I can make it all right."

Glacia braced, readying the card between her fingers... Axiss about-faced and hurtled off the roof head over heels. Glacia rushed to the edge, her face registering the horror.

***

Fatal, Hoodrat and Fatalianika whisked the last few stragglers out of the courtyard when the sound of clicking heels echoed behind them, getting closer. They turned to find Jordyn Martinez approaching.

"Get outta here, Mami," Fatal said. "It's not safe here."

"Apparently, it's not safe anywhere on the planet," Jordyn said. "But I think the safest place is with the people here to save it. You're Johnny Fatal and Hoodrat, right?"

"Who is you?" Hoodrat asked with a ghetto-girl neck-roll.

"Jordyn Martinez, WPHZ News --"

"-- Ain't no soundbites here, yo," Fatal said. "Do us a favor. Get lost." The trio resumed moving across the courtyard.

"I know about the Von Pyros clone!" Jordyn yelled. The trio froze in their tracks. Jordyn trotted back up to them.

"Tucci disclosed to me everything," Jordyn said. "The disappearances, intergalactic trade, Wrath the Conqueror's return... He was scheduled to go public with it on my show this morning. I guess Von Pyros got to the poor bastard first."

Hoodrat sniffed the air, her olfactory sense picking up the stench of metals and body odors. She whirled just in time to see a handful of SWAT agents in the shadows poised to fire. "Watch out!"

The agents opened fire. Jordyn took cover behind a nearby dumpster. Fatal tattooed himself to the ground just as a barrage of bullets pinged across him. He made his arms and Glocks tangible, capped two agents and tossed a grenade -- KABOOM! Fatal then flowed across the ground into an alcove and through the doors of City Hall behind Hoodrat and Fatalianika.

"Y'all ah-ight?" Fatal asked, his adrenaline pumping high from the hairy thrill. No answer. He looked over. Hoodrat was closing Fatalianika's vacantly staring eyes as she became consumed by death, a pool of blood seeping from under her. Fatal's tattooed physicality slid from the floor up the wall.

"Go ahead, yo," Fatal said grimly. "I'll take care of them."

Hoodrat looked at Fatal sullenly, the whole scenario reminding her of Kataklysmo's fate. She planted a departing kiss on his subsistence on the wall then took off down the hallway and vanished around a corner.

Fatal edged off the wall slightly to peek at the smattering of agents closing in on the entrance. He drew a breath then reached for the rocket launcher tattoo on his shoulder…

The entrance door suddenly shattered as teargas grenades and gunfire riddled the corridor. Gas and smoke rolled through, followed by flurries of movement and agents swarming in.

Through fogged visuals, an agent looked back and caught a glimpse of a figure poised with a rocket launcher over his shoulder -- KABOOM! The rocket's sudden blast tore through the corridor as Johnny Fatal annihilated the surprised life out of them.

More agents emerging. Fatal lunged, tattooing himself to a wall just as bullets stitched across him. He then began pumping out shells as fast as he could squeeze the triggers.

In the chaos, Guerrilla leaped out of an agent just as the body was riddled with bullets. Guerrilla phased inside of another agent, then another and another and another, leaving a trail of dead agents behind him.

Fatal threw down a flash grenade, its illuminated burst concealing him as he slid across the decimated entrance back into City Hall.

After a moment, a lone agent emerged and followed behind him into the building…

***

Hoodrat scuttled up City Hall's spiraling staircase, the sounds of war turning into silence behind her. Her ears pricked acutely from a sound a few landings up, like wood screeching on a marble floor. She quickly scampered up the steps.

Hoodrat emerged on the sixth floor and saw the clone of Von Pyros reclining on a wooden bench. His jacket and tie were off and his shirt was open, revealing his chest-eye.

"Why you sittin' here all by yourself?" Hoodrat asked as she neared. Von Pyros didn't say a word, but his soulless gaze communicated exactly what he wanted.

"Here?" Hoodrat asked as she sat next to him capriciously. "What if we get caught?"

Von Pyros leaned in, his breath grazing the nape of her neck. Hoodrat sighed deeply, as if it was her first time.

"It would be kind of freaky, though."

THIRTY-SEVEN

FATAL SHADES OF LIGHT

Emosha and Shadowstar mixed it up in a fierce sword-wielding battle that waged on top of and around concrete benches, the famous LOVE statue and the high-spouting memorial fountain.

Emosha charged forward with a ferocious attack. Shadowstar countered and delivered an iron-palm strike to Emosha's chest, knocking her back. Still on her feet, Emosha turned invisible. She then staged an imperceptible slash-fest from all angles.

As Shadowstar reeled, he caught a glimpse of Mister Mystiqal streaking toward them from high above. He then glanced sharply at a passing helicopter, its shadow on a building lining up adjacent to Mystiqal. With his eyes locked on the helicopter's shadow, Shadowstar scampered away and fly-kicked through a shadow on a building, disappearing --

-- Shadowstar emerged out of the helicopter's shadow, his leg fully extended. He landed a perfectly-timed face-distorting kick to Mystiqal, knocking him out of the sky, onto the high-spouting fountain and into its knee-deep pool --

-- Shadowstar's trajectory forced him to drop into a shadowy area on the opposite building. He then rolled out of a shadow near the ground and resumed fighting Emosha without missing a beat.

Shadowstar pressed his attack. Emosha expertly blocked and countered, unleashing a fast and furious assault, driving him back. Shadowstar was game but losing. He ducked in and out of shadows and snuck a hit in on occasion, but Emosha's string of formidable striking techniques forced him to retreat and vanish indefinitely into the shadows.

Emosha cat-stepped forward as she surveyed the shadowy facades critically. Trusting nothing within her super-optic faculties, she unsheathed a bow and arrow. Aligning the arrow and pulling the bowstring taut, she closed her eyes and posed in frozen concentration, trying to "feel" Shadowstar's next manifestation.

After a tense moment of idleness, Emosha whirled and let the arrow fly. With a thunk, the arrow penetrated and lodged deep into the shaded area of a news van. Shadowstar staggered out of the shaded abyss and fell to his knees, his chest skewered by the arrow. Emosha reloaded her bow and aimed with deadly enmity. Shadowstar hesitated then crumbled to the ground, dead.

Emosha concealed her bow then headed to the fountain where Mystiqal was surfacing on the side of the pool. His costume was soaked through to the skin and strands of hair clung to his face. He looked like he had the mange.

"I am the foremost exponent of the mystic arts on the planet," Mystiqal said between gasps and wheezes. "How does this keep happening to me?"

Emosha almost smiled. She bolstered him out of the pool and they then proceeded to head toward City Hall, with Mister Mystiqal dripping all the way.

***

A lone agent moved down the City Hall corridor, his eyes constantly moving. Suddenly he stopped and looked to the marble floor beneath him. A double flash of steel --

Bullets suddenly ripped through the agent's underside, blasting him to death. His body dropped beside Fatal's smoke-wisping glocks sticking out from the floor. Fatal detached his body from the floor and stood over the agent's body a moment.

A sharp metal click sound behind him. Fatal whirled to find the muzzle of Guerrilla's gun jammed tight to his head --

BOOM! The gunshot blast speared the air. Hoodrat dismissed it as she shimmied her pants up past her hips. Von Pyros was off to the side, buckling his pants.

"Short but sweet," Hoodrat said. "Don't worry about it. Happens to a lot of guys. The good news is..." Hoodrat scratched open a gateway as she talked in a sing-songy voice, "There's somebody that wants to meet you."

Von Pyros' attention lifted as a low guttural growl came from within the gateway. He moved closer, enthralled by a barely discernible figure in the darkness, its yellow eyes glowing eerily...

***

Earth Angel was planted at the edge of a rooftop, looking down on Wrath as he dismantled demons in a zealous frenzy.

"The earth is not just plants and the four elements," Earth Angel said aloud, calling to mind Wrath's words to dream big and take chances with his powers. He took a deep breath and raised his hand grandly. The air hummed with ions and electrons and formed into a lightning bolt in his grasp. Then like a latter-day Zeus, Earth Angel hurled it down at a police car that exploded, taking out a swarm of demons.

Empowered, Earth Angel stretched out his wings and leaped off the building. Cement and asphalt began to rush up from the earth to meet him, encasing his body. He whooshed down and socked a demon with his now concrete fists.

Landing in the middle of a demonic horde, Earth Angel exploded out of the rock formation strikingly, bombarding them with deadly rubble. Then with two crackling shafts of electrical energy, Earth Angel proceeded to hack through the demonic battalion, scorching their insides with each whack of high voltage.

Seeing Earth Angel's joy with his newly adopted abilities, Wrath soared away, leaving him to dispatch the dozen or so demons left. He then sailed into the entrance of City Hall.

THIRTY-EIGHT

PR⊙GENY

Wrath the Conqueror glided through City Hall into the lobby's immense clock tower just as a wounded scream echoed from above. He blazed up the tower, emerged onto the sixth-floor corridor and beheld a horrific sight --

THE HULKING FEMALE PROGENY OF THE VON PYROS' CLONE AND HOODRAT was sucking on Hoodrat's jugular with voracious fervor. Rat-like and covered primarily with dense fur, Progeny's chest-eye resided between eggplant-shaped breasts and her claws were comprised of kindling spectral flames. Progeny tore a strip of Hoodrat's shirt then flung her like a rag doll near Wrath's feet.

Wrath kneeled to Hoodrat's crumpled body, her neck ravaged and bloody. Hoodrat angled to him and spoke in a choked gurgle.

"H-How...come y-you...you never...tried to h-holla at me..." Hoodrat's voice faded as she expelled her last breath, her insatiable lust a tool for her own demise.

"Hoodrat wasn't born a hoe, she was made, unknowingly programmed since grammar school," Progeny said with a guttural timbre. "Everything we've done had a contingent effect. We left nothing to chance." Progeny stepped closer with a lecherous sneer, revealing her blood-flecked fangs. "But I couldn't let Hoodrat live, knowing we both wanted the same baby daddy... could I?"

Wrath stood to his full authoritative height; his face twisted with contempt. In an explosion of fury, he let his hands go, throwing telekinetic punches. Progeny slipped the esoteric blows like a defensive boxing wizard. Wrath was stunned. "I'm not Vampyro."

Progeny teleported behind Wrath and force-blasted -- he crashed through a wall into an empty courtroom and thwacked to the jury box with debilitating impact. Progeny scurried through the freshly made hole, straddled on top of Wrath and roughly shoved the cloth into his mouth. "You gonna give me my baby..."

***

In the City Hall courtyard, Jordyn emerged from behind the dumpster just in time to see Von Pyros and a host of ambassadors being rushed by security into a fleet of government cars.

Barely missing the motorcade as they pulled off, Glacia, Earth Angel, Emosha and Mister Mystiqal traipsed up to the demolished entrance. Jordyn adjusted her course and filed into the building behind them.

As they entered the City Hall lobby, faint thuds averted their heads skyward. Glacia waved Jordyn off as the squad ascended the spiral staircase, with Emosha at point...

***

Still in the cowgirl position, Progeny unloaded a series of diabolical scratches that seared Wrath's flesh. He writhed wildly, his eyes screaming in excruciating pain. Gagged and on the brink of unconsciousness, all Wrath could do was watch Progeny as she forged ahead with her defilement, reaching beneath herself to unbuckle his pants...

As the darkness began to close in on him, Wrath's consciousness rocketed through City Hall at the nano speed of thought. It careened down the stairwell towards the four murky figures of the Children of the Apocalypse. Three of the figures completely faded, leaving only one: Emosha. Wrath's consciousness plunged into her --

-- Emosha's eyes trembled as a sudden chill shuddered through her, possessing her soul with pure rage. With a barbarous scream, an aura of fury exploded outward from her, disturbing the emotions of Glacia, Earth Angel and Mister Mystiqal. Enraged, they charged up the stairs...

Everything dimmed as Wrath expelled the last of his strength. The last thing he saw was Progeny's trance-like face bobbing rhythmically on top of him.

Galloping feet and crazed yells averted Progeny's attention, getting louder as they neared. Progeny rolled off Wrath just as the door smashed open. Emosha, Glacia, Earth Angel and Mister Mystiqal stampeded down the aisle in an emotional state of savage fury.

Without hesitation, Progeny erected a force field that sizzled from the barrage of photon stars, ice-etched cards, fire blasts and mystic bolts, but stayed up.

Eager to reassert his presumed superiority, Mister Mystiqal teleported and boldly materialized on the other side of the force field next to Progeny. With inhuman speed, Progeny seized him by the throat.

"Such a pathetic waste of talent," Progeny snarled as arctic-fire from her claws spread rapidly from Mystiqal's neck, artery-like. It consumed his entire body, vanquishing him into a husk of cinders. Progeny dusted her hands of Mystiqal's charred remains like the crumbs of a sandwich. All were horrified.

Earth Angel narrowed his eyes, concentrating his gaze beneath Progeny's feet. The marble floor began to heat and liquify, sinking her. In a panic, Progeny dropped the force field and floundered as if she was submerging in quicksand. Earth Angel extracted the heat and the floor re-solidified, trapping her bicep deep. He then punctuated his trapping with a lightning bolt. Progeny roared.

The apocalyptic trio then charged forward savagely. Progeny inhaled heavily, steeling herself -- KABOOM! Progeny exploded out of the floor, crashing everyone hard to the level below in a hail of fragmented wood and chunks of flooring.

Suddenly there was stillness within the haze of wafting dust. After a moment, Glacia stirred, her body cut, scraped and wracked with pain. Gathering the will to move, she rolled to her knees and spotted Wrath nearby flattened on a bed of debris. He was horribly bruised, and the cloth was still lodged in his mouth. Glacia frantically crawled toward Wrath --

A large hideous foot suddenly slammed down in front of her followed by the other. Her eyes traveled upward to the beastly figure of Progeny.

"He's mine, bitch," Progeny said, "You just in the way." Progeny tensed her hand, her fiery claws poised to strike --

A masculine hand suddenly grabbed her wrist. Progeny half-turned and saw a glimpse of Kinetis just before a metallic fist zoomed into her visual field at an accelerated rate --

KA-POW! Kinetis smashed Progeny with a powerhouse punch that sent her flying. She crashed through the wall on the other side of the room... the sound of another wall... then another... and another... and another.

Kinetis, now wearing camouflage warpaint on the fleshly parts of his face, turned to the figure of Emosha drifting over to him. She stared at him a moment, her look of respect and attraction dissolving into just giving him a cool dap.

The duo pivoted to the sounds of crackling rubble. Earth Angel was crawling from underneath remnants of ceiling and floor, his wings spackled with blood. Kinetis and Emosha rushed to his aid.

As they bolstered Earth Angel up, he looked over to find Glacia solemnly removing the cloth from Wrath's mouth, his body maimed and lifeless. Earth Angel broke free and knelt with Glacia. He listened for breaths and checked for pulse, desperately searching Wrath for signs of life... Nothing.

Glacia stared at Wrath a disoriented moment, his mortality hitting her like a ton of bricks. Then her expression faded into the most remarkable compassion. Kinetis, Emosha and Earth Angel watched in profound silence as Glacia made a heartfelt plea to arouse Wrath somehow and her tears were a testament of that hope.

"You put a song in my heart the first day I met you," Glacia said. "Whether together or apart, you have been my best friend, my rock, my foundation. A Savior to the whole world but a gift, made especially for me. I don't believe you've come this far to leave me."

Earth Angel swallowed hard as he stood slowly, barely holding it together. He gently grabbed Glacia by the shoulders and helped her to rise. As he escorted her away, Glacia looked back to Wrath and emptied the remaining words of conviction within her soul.

"It's time for the eagle to rise above the storm."

Glacia hesitated a moment then turned and assembled with the rest of her team, unaware of the significant power of her affirmation. Wrath's fingers slightly twitched as his wounds slowly begin to shrink and heal...

"Bet we get blamed for all of this," Emosha said, breaking the doleful mood.

"We'll just tell people the truth," Kinetis said.

"You're not unplugged yet?" Earth Angel barked. "Nobody will believe --"

Progeny suddenly rushed in and charged into Kinetis with the titanic force of a freight train, startling everyone off their feet. Kinetis hurtled through the air and crashed through the window and beyond. Before anyone could react, Progeny force blasted. Earth Angel and Emosha smacked hard against a wall and fell, stunned.

Glacia ice-blasted in rapid-fire succession. Evading, Progeny blurred forward, seized Glacia one-handed by the throat and lifted her off the ground...

THIRTY-NINE

LYRICS OF FURY

The armada of government cars arrived at a heliport at Penns Landing, situated on the Delaware River. Von Pyros and the dignitaries exited the cars and headed toward a few helicopters awaiting take-off.

Brotherhood of the Vampyrians czars were quickly ushered into the helicopters. An assistant escorted a shaken Lilith into a loaded helicopter then stood vigil beside Von Pyros, leaving the rest of the dignitaries standing there, bewildered.

"Where are the rest of helicopters?" The African delegate queried. "Surely not everyone will fit."

A Kindred representative looked from the helicopters to Guerrilla stepping out of Lilith's assistant, aiming his hand-cannon at the dignitaries. "It's a double-cross."

"What did you expect from the architect of deception?" Von Pyros said. "Goodbye. See you soon. In Hell."

Guerrilla sprayed. The aide and the dignitaries fell, dead. Von Pyros and Guerrilla then boarded a helicopter...

***

Jordyn moved down the City Hall corridor and neared the decimated office, the muted sounds of violence bringing her to the breaking point of fear. She forced herself to look in the room and stopped dead in her tracks. Glacia was squirming in Progeny's grasp like a captured fish. Jordyn was powerless.

Progeny accented her torment with a villainous monologue, but Glacia wasn't digesting any of Progeny's prattling, her sensations dulled by the life that was being choked out of her.

Suddenly, an unnatural windchill picked up as debris fragments swirled around the room.

Jordyn looked over, her jaw dropping in awe --

Glacia's eyes veered and brightened with a look of hope --

Progeny looked over as if she was seeing a ghost. "No --"

Across the room, Wrath the Conqueror was standing with an extraordinarily mythic look, his locks pendulating slightly as he bobbed his head as if to a beat, assembling his thoughts.

"Yeah...unh..."

Progeny tossed Glacia aside and charged through the cosmic wind toward Wrath with deadly purpose.

"Stay right there, muthafucka," Wrath commanded, freezing Progeny in her tracks. **"I'm about to put your Mercury in retrograde with that real talk... I'ma destroy your ass..."**

And then, Wrath just went off, freestyling. Rage disguised as melodious lyrics exploded out of his mouth. Stentorian. Epic.

Destructive. With the cadence of Notorious B.I.G.'s "Ready To Die", Wrath's words carried with it an etheric vibration that attacked Progeny with a physical effect as his rhyme flow became the physical manifestation of his name:

"As I start to rap, particles in your brain cells
travel through your veins, blood vessels start to swell
Words absorbed through your pores, whore,
I know that you feel it, Wrath the Conqueror,
snatching your mind, soul, body and spirit
Metaphors are carnivorous from the great chivalrous
rhyme spitter, Dyme hitter, the atom splitter,
I bend space and time on some fly shit
My tongue's the paradigm shift that upset demonic
schemes, ancestor's best when I wreck shit
Inflections infecting, dissecting
My tone and timbre give you a seizure and diarrhea
Fiend, you burning from my lyrical gonnorhea, huh
My verses heavy, so heavy I had to drop, see?
It is written, so nobody can stop me
Rhymes pound with the sound of the double barrel
as my flow corrodes then explodes in your bone
marrow,
It's the Conqueror..."

Wrath's esoteric wordplay caused Progeny's head to swell and pulsate. She grabbed the sides of her skull as agonizing pains ricocheted through her like a pinball. Diseased particles began to eat away at her body tissue, creating patterned holes of energy that slashed across her body and face. Progeny collapsed to the floor and writhed seizurally as more holes of energy burst through, consuming her, the intensity rising...

Sensing the inevitability, Glacia grabbed Jordyn and hunkered with Earth Angel and Emosha, projecting a fortified ice-dwelling over them...

And then, with an inhuman cry of anguish, Progeny's physical form went nova, exploding with tremendous force. Windows were blown outward as the concussive tide of energy blew Wrath's clothes and locs back amid flying shrapnel.

Heaps of evil spirits withered away amid clouds of dust and smoke. No one could have survived that. Except Wrath the Conqueror. He strode through the phantasmic energy like the God that he was, occult wisps trailing.

Wrath panned around. Glacia, Emosha, Earth Angel and Jordyn were looming from the dissipating igloo. Wrath then produced a blunt.

"Spark." The blunt lit upon his command. He took a couple of hits then offered the weed to any takers. Earth Angel reached for it and puffed, his virgin lungs forcing him to cough unceasingly.

Kinetis emerged into the room, amped and ready for war. He stopped short, calmed by the subdued tableau before him.

"I'm glad that's over," Kinetis said, handing Lilith's unique deck of tarot cards to Wrath.

"That was just foreplay," Wrath said. "But there are thousands of warriors in the struggle. Some ready to fight. Some we gotta enlighten. But they're out there." Wrath then turned to Jordyn. "Document everything that you've seen and heard. Tell it. Let it be known from the highest heights to the deepest depths... Wrath the Conqueror is back, baby."

The sounds of nearing sirens diverted everyone's attention out the window.

"What now?" Earth Angel coughed out.

"Fall back, dawg," Wrath said as he focused on the departing government helicopters off in the distance that became a handful of specks, shrinking into nothingness. "Time to fall back."

Wrath then generated a tempestuous storm that clouded the room. The storm abated and dissipated...

Jordyn Martinez looked around, stunned. Wrath the Conqueror and the Children of the Apocalypse were gone.